INSTANT REPLAYS OF THE EXODUS

A NOVEL

CHRISTOPHER P. GAZEENT

For Austin Martell

CONTENTS

"Too much joy, I swear, is lost
in our desperation to keep it."
—Ocean Vuong

PROLOGUE

Tuesday, August 1, 2006

There is a town in upstate New York, an ordinary, affluent suburb by anyone's measure, called Quincy. It's a typical suburban town. There are houses, some of them on hills. There's a high school right in the middle of town. There's a café. And there's a diner.

On Tuesday, August 1, 2006, 4 young men sat around a table at the diner.

"I'd like to write a novel about us someday," said one of them, a guy with a shock of fire-red hair. "This needs documenting. You know, *us.*"

"For sure, Mistah Red," said one of the others. He was somewhat overweight with ear length, very dark hair.

"This is our culture, Jim," said Red. "Who knows if there's anything as pure as this anywhere in the world? This diner. Our youth."

"Well, anyway," said the third, "we're here for a very specific purpose." He was very thin with a skull and bones beanie.

"You're right, Bones, my friend," said Jim. He took a deep breath and counted off, "One, two, three!"

And Red, Jim, and Bones sang together off-key, "Happy birthday to you, happy birthday to you! Happy birthday, dear Ox, happy birthday to you! May you live 100 years, may you drink 1 million beers! Get plastered, you bastard, happy birthday to you!"

Ox smiled meekly. "Thanks, guys." He had short brown hair and was dressed all in black.

"How does 15 feel?" asked Red.

"Oh, you know, not much different from 14," said Ox. "The inexorable march toward adulthood. I imagine 18 will be fun. And 21. After that, who knows? Perhaps one is better off not seeing 22 and beyond."

"Oh, don't say that," said Bones. "I want to be friends with all you guys for a very long time. Barring something unforeseen."

"It's true, people drift apart sometimes," said Red. "But right now, we're here. Let's soak this in. Even if memories end up being all we have."

"None of us can predict the future," said Jim. "But if you do write a novel, maybe that's all we'll need by the time we're gone."

"That's my intention."

PART ONE: ZBIGNIEW

A. A BOY CALLED RED

1. The Redmobile, Part 1

Saturday, February 29, 2020

I went to pick up Annie from her house in Mt. Kisco. She was already at the door of the condo, dressed in the red dress she'd specifically bought for the event. "We match!" she exclaimed delightedly.

"Ah, yes," I said. My tie was the same color.

"Give us a hug," she said, and I hugged her. Then we kissed.

"Off we go to the Redmobile!" she cried. She followed me down the stairs to the ring of sorts around which cars were parked.

"Check out my parallel parking job. First try. Pretty good, huh?"

"Oh, yeah," she said. "Nice and tight."

I unlocked the driver's side door, then pressed the button to unlock the whole vehicle. Annie climbed into the passenger seat. The back of the car was filled with boxes of old miscellania, which made it difficult to carry any more passengers outside of the front seat. Occasionally her brother Kevin asked for a ride somewhere and he just had to squeeze in.

"You said this wedding is at Briarcliff Manor? Or was it in Briarcliff Manor?"

"Both," I said. "That's where it is, and that's the name of the venue."

I started the car and put it into gear. Then I exited the complex and we set off for the place. We rode in silence through the suburbia of Westchester. We weren't far from the college where we'd met long ago.

"Any progress on the story?" she finally asked.

"Not really," I said glumly. "I don't know if I'll ever finish a novel. Fifty thousand words, I mean."

"Well, not everyone can write the Great American Novel."

"I guess not."

"At least you have plenty of time to work on it."

Dead silence. It had snowed the previous day and the sides of the road were coated in whiteness that reflected the bright sunlight of the early afternoon. I always found white snow and blue sky incongruous. If it was going to be snowy, I preferred a nice, austere gray sky.

"How was your week, anyway?" I asked.

"Tiring. We have this one difficult child named Timmy, and yesterday he fucking punched the head teacher in the nose."

"What?"

"Yeah. It was around naptime, and he got cranky."

"Yikes."

"I mean, it's not like it could have even hurt that much. Oh! I caught another shiny!"

"Congrats. I haven't encountered any."

We were talking about the latest Pokémon games, gen eight. I let her go on about it, half-listening. I played the games too, but I wasn't nearly as obsessive about the whole thing as she was.

"Oh, and Kev has been visiting this weekend," she continued. "Meaning the place reeks of weed."

"Can't he smoke that shit outside?"

"You'd think."

"Hmm."

Then she told me all about a new anime coming out that she was excited about. Soon we reached the place. It was fancy. A valet took my car.

We walked in. There was that expectant buzz felt in the lobby of a building where 2 people were about to get married. Suits and dresses milled about, socializing with one another. I fiddled with my tie.

"Red?" I looked to see who was there.

"Hey, Casper!" I stuck out my hand, and he shook it. "Haven't seen you in forever."

"This is my wife, Jen," he said, and I shook her hand in the gentle way a man shakes a woman's hand, a squeeze almost. She was pregnant.

"This is my plus-one, Annie," I said, and she waved at them enthusiastically.

Casper got distracted by someone else. Annie and I made our way through the crowd. Then I saw someone else I knew. "Olivia?" I asked hesitantly.

"Zbigniew!" she cried and gave me a hug. She was wearing a very sparkly green dress that went down to her ankles.

"Didn't you always call me Red?"

She paused and thought. "I think I called you both."

"Well, it's great to see you."

Olivia and I parted.

"Have you ever noticed," I remarked to Annie, "that there's much more creativity in formal wear for the female persuasion? All the men here are wearing the same damn suit. All we get to play around with is our ties."

We walked over to the table on which the seating cards were laid out. As I was looking for mine, I noticed something and froze.

"What's up?" Annie asked.

"Jim Paciullo," I said very quietly. I hadn't seen him in the lobby. Then, I said, "Oh, God. I hope Bones isn't here."

I found my seating card: ZBIGNIEW WOJCIK. All spelled correctly, astoundingly.

After milling about and recognizing more people I hadn't seen in forever, we were all ushered into the wedding hall. The various members of the wedding party entered the room, all choreographed to a lively pop tune that I couldn't quite place, concluding with Amanda and Jack, the bride and groom. I looked at the groomsmen and sure enough, there was Jim. He had a big beard covering his face now, but it was him for sure.

The wedding went the way they do. Various speeches were made, culminating in the "I dos", at which point Annie turned and looked at me, with the expression made when something cute happens.

Importantly, there was no sight of Bones.

There was a cocktail hour. I sipped my beloved rum daisy. No bartender ever seemed to know what it was, so I always had to instruct them: two parts rum, one part lemon juice, a good dash of grenadine. I could feel the blood vessels in my esophagus opening up as a warm feeling overcame me.

At one point, I spotted Jim across the room from me, unoccupied. I walked purposefully over to him and shouted, "Jim!" He gave me one of his huge hugs, enveloping me to the point where I could hardly breathe. I was relieved: I half thought he wouldn't want to see me, after everything that had happened back in the day.

"How have you been?" I asked.

"Good," he said, and although he was the same person, the word coming from his mouth had an air of disconnect to it, as if I could never truly know him any longer. "And you?"

"Good, too." There was a brief awkward silence. "Well, nice to see you." I went back over to where Annie sat. She was drinking a colorful beverage.

Cocktail hour ended, and then there was dinner. I asked for the salmon; Annie the chicken. The food took what felt like an eternity to arrive. After eating, we were the first to leave, heading out right after we finished our meals. I did not care for dancing, and Annie knew that.

I got my car from the valet and we began the drive back to Mt. Kisco. "Why didn't I talk to him more?" I bemoaned to Annie.

"Your friend?"

"Yes. Jim. I should've at least asked him what he's been up to. And when will I see him again now? The next wedding? The next funeral, for God's sake?"

There were a couple moments of quiet. "I love you," she said.

"I love you, too."

I dropped her off at her condo and headed back to my house in Quincy. When I arrived, I eagerly tore off my suit. How strange to have seen him. How sad that I would never really know him again.

2. Seven Years Ago

Sunday, June 19, 2016

It's been 7 years since I've seen Jim Paciullo, and I don't know if I'll ever see him again. If I do, he probably wouldn't want to see me.

I remember the instant message from Sven: "Hey, Red… I've been asked to tell you something."

"Yeah?" I already knew what it was.

"*sigh* Oh boy. Uh… Susan doesn't want you coming to her house anymore."

"I figured you'd say that. I guess I don't need you to tell me why."

"Look, Red," Sven continued anyway. "Attending a party to which you have not been invited is known as crashing and is generally frowned upon. We saw you eating communal guacamole with your fingers. You slept on the kitchen floor the other morning, and nobody could make you budge. And you told us you were glad Bones and Kayla's grandmother had died so you could get a ride to Faire. Which, regardless of malicious intent, is just… cruel."

Well, that was pretty damning. I winced.

"If you want to know the truth, Bones said you're an insensitive asshole. And… yes, you behaved insensitively. You acted like an asshole. But you are not an insensitive asshole. And I'm willing to remain friends with you."

I remember feeling like everyone in the world hated me. I didn't go to bed that night. I stayed up and took a long walk under the full moon. The air spoke of anguish and disillusionment. I felt like crying, but I didn't.

3. Goodbye, Cruel World

Wednesday, 17 December, 2014

"Dear Everyone,

It's hard not to imagine the reaction there will be once I'm gone. Part of me wants to say, "Yes, now they will realize. Everyone will say, Oh, why didn't we see this coming? The signs were all there!" But I don't want to be smug in my death. Really, I'm just done. Done with every day feeling like surgery without anesthesia.

So, I wish I could say I was sorry. But I know you'll all be better off without me. And I realize too that that's such a stereo-typical thing for a depressed patient to say. But I can't shake it. I don't deserve any of you.

The only person I'll miss is Red, for reasons that should be obvious. Besides that, I believe there's peace in oblivion. Every night I wait for the warmth of the covers to envelop me. Every morning, I wish I'd died in my sleep.

People always say that you shouldn't kill yourself because think of all the things in your future you'll be missing out on! But I am in the opposite corner: If I had done this 5 years ago, think of all the trouble I could've avoided!

Sincerely,

Ox"

4. Mr. Parsons

Monday, May 28, 2012

"It's nice to meet you, Mr. Parsons," Annie said, shaking my father's hand. He looked at her in confusion as I looked at her in annoyance.

"You can call him Norm," I muttered, and my father laughed as though he'd suddenly thought of something funny.

"Well, it's nice to meet you too, Annie. Of course, I've heard about you from Z—"

"*Please!*" I interrupted.

He laughed again. "You mean you haven't told her your real name yet?"

"I've told her that it's unusual, and that it begins with a letter near the end of the alphabet. That's enough, and that's that."

"Oh, is that that, Mr. That's That?" he responded in a nasal voice.

"Stop quoting *Family Guy*," I said. Then to Annie, I said, "He likes to try to quote *Family Guy*."

She looked around. "Big place."

"Yes, yes," I said hurriedly. "I suppose I should show you around."

I showed her the living room, the kitchen, and my bedroom, all of which were small, bordering on cramped. "This is the old part of the house. It was built in the 1930s."

Then I showed her the family room, and upstairs, the studio. It was a huge room. "Then this part my dad built in the early '80s, after my parents moved up from Brooklyn."

"So does he still paint up here?"

"Sadly, no. He did some stained glass recently, but that's about it."

"Why, what happened?"

I didn't feel like telling her the whole sob story of my parents' divorce and my father's mental breakdown, so I just said, "He lost interest."

We lingered in the studio. The walls were covered in canvas. My father's paintings were abstract. In one there was a huge bird flying over a landscape of bright checkered colors. In another there were a number of hearts with halos, some right side up, others upside down. I reflected that there were a great many people who would be happy living in the square footage of such a room.

5. Hair

Saturday, August 27, 2011

"I LOVE YOUR HAIR!"

I turned around to see who was shouting at me. I saw a girl with medium-length brown hair and bangs, along with a woman and a young boy, her mother and brother, I presumed, and a Pomeranian.

She ran up to me. "Ooh, can I touch it?"

"Sure," I said, and she brushed her hand on the top of my red mohawk.

"I'm Annie, by the way."

"Red here. You know, because of the hair."

"It's glorious," she said.

"So, are you moving in today?"

"Yes, naturally, and you?"

"Yes. Speaking of which, I was on the way to my dorm room to finish setting my stuff up. But let's maybe meet up later?"

"How does Starby's sound?"

We exchanged phone numbers. Later, we agreed to meet at the on-campus Starbucks at 2 p.m. I ordered an almond milk latte. When they asked my name for the order, I said, "Stanisław." The guy behind the counter didn't exactly pronounce it correctly when he repeated it back to me, but whatever. She ordered a matcha tea.

"So that was your family before?" I asked.

"Yes, that was my mom, and my brother, Kevin, and our dog, Cleopatra."

"Nice. I'm here with my dad."

"Are you excited about the new games?" She had a way of cutting right to the chase. I knew right away she meant Pokémon.

"I've sort of fallen off the wagon with that, to be quite honest," I said.

"Oh, too bad," she said.

Our drinks were ready ("Annie and… Stan?") and we grabbed them and sat down at a table.

She started telling me all about a Pokémon theme park in Tokyo as we sipped. She wanted to visit Japan one day. I caught myself fantasizing about going with her as she continued to talk. I watched her mouth moving and her face gesticulating as she excitedly reported the details, and I knew she was something special, although I wasn't sure yet in what capacity.

6. My Father

2015:

"Son, how the FUCK can I care about a Mets score when I have lost thousands of dollars today?" my dad yelled as he slammed his whiskey glass down on the old wooden table. "I tell you time and again, professional sports are the opiate of the people. They exist to distract people from what's really going on."

2023:

"So, Dad, my portfolio went down 1.03% today."

"Well, yes, because the Fed has its head up its ass and…"

Now I'm speaking his language. It's sad that it took the mother of his son getting sick and dying and my investing the inheritance. Conclusion: It's a lot healthier to care about something that *doesn't* matter, like baseball.

7. Back in the Day

Friday, June 12, 2009

The bell rang. Blessed freedom! Before Friday ended though, it was time for chess club. I got up from my senior history desk and grabbed my backpack, then headed upstairs to the language department.

"Rossotino!" exclaimed Señor Mecca as I entered. I was the 1st there. I took Italian, and "Rossotino" is an Italian diminutive for red, like "Reddy" almost. He told me often that he had always regretted not having had me as a student, but I'd spurned Spanish when the decision came out of a fear of mindless conformity. It seemed everyone else was doing it. So Italian it was.

"Oh… can I show you something?" he asked, suddenly sounding deflated. "Come over here."

I came to his desk. He pulled out an official looking printout and pointed at it. I saw my name. "Do you know what this is?"

I had a feeling I did. "The ineligible list?"

"Yes, the ineligible list, and there you are, Zbigniew Wojcik." He sighed. "Don't worry. I won't tell anyone. You can still come to the chess club. But please, tell me, how did this happen?"

"I'm kind of failing English."

"Failing English? But young man… not to butter you up, but you are brilliant. Why are you failing English?"

"I didn't feel like doing the term paper."

He sighed again. "Well, I won't prod any further. But I must admit I'm disappointed."

I felt terrible. Señor Mecca was my buddy. I'd known him for four years and we burned prog rock CDs for one another.

Then three guys entered the room. "Jim! Bones! Ox!" the teacher greeted them.

"Señor Mecca! Red!" Jim shouted. He walked over to the desk and gave me an enormous hug that left me suffocated.

I waved at Bones and Ox. Bones grinned at me. Ox looked at the ground. I suddenly remembered the scene from 3 years ago: "And this one," Jim had said. "Always standing at the edge of the circle awkwardly. The awkward one. Awks. Ox!"

It had stuck, just like Red had when I started dyeing my hair red in 8th grade. I don't remember who started calling me that, but I don't believe it was Jim's responsibility.

Gradually, the others made their way in. The club consisted of a loose group of friends who all hung out by the Four Doors before school started. Everyone had known one another for years now, but I didn't feel any great loyalty to them, except for Jim, Bones and Ox. Those were my buds.

We set up the chess sets. I was decent at chess, not great, but the social aspect was the point. Jim wore blue jeans and a T-shirt that said, "I come from the island of misfit toys." Bones wore a Jack Skellington T-shirt and a black beanie with a skull and bones on it. Ox wore all black.

I got in three or four games. I was able to beat my classmates, but Señor Mecca mercilessly kicked my ass, as usual.

We all lined up at the teacher's desk to collect our late bus passes. They were yellow that day. Then we headed outside to wait for the bus. It was a beautiful June day, warm and sunny. There wouldn't be many more of these gatherings of friends before we graduated, or didn't graduate, as the case may have been. I'd stuck out the year with my buddies, but I knew I'd be skipping graduation. It wasn't a big deal. All I had to do was get my GED and then I'd go to WCC for a while, then I could go somewhere else.

We boarded the old school bus and headed to the back, as usual. Jim pulled out an iPod and little speakers. "What'll it be today, dudes?"

"Clan of Xymox," Ox requested.

Jim laughed. "Okay. One song." He put on "A Day," which played as the bus started up and headed out of the parking lot onto the road.

When it ended, Jim said, "You know what it's time for?"

"'Fat Bottomed Girls'?" I asked.

"'Fat Bottomed Girls,'" Jim said in assent and nodded. He put it on. After a few minutes, the time had come. Brian May's guitar paused momentarily, then Jim shouted in unison with Freddie Mercury, "GET ON YOUR BIKES AND RIDE!" It was a ritual.

I was the first to be dropped off. I gave my friends hugs and then walked up the long dirt driveway to my house. There would be so few more of these gatherings, so few chess clubs to come, Fridays, rides on the late bus, Jim screaming *get on your bikes and ride.* I was 18 years old, and I had no idea what my future would hold. The past and future were intermingling, resulting in a confused and transitory present. All I could do was enjoy the nice weather.

8. In the City

Friday, October 1, 2021

"And I don't think I told you about Dragon Man," he said as he took a puff of the joint.

"Dragon Man?" she laughed.

"Yes, Helen. He was a scalie."

"What does that even mean, Kev?"

They strolled through Washington Square Park, approaching the fountain. Autumn was coming on and it was an unusually cool evening, and Kevin was wearing a black cloak over his mesh shirt, gray pants and tall boots.

"Jeez, you really are new to this, aren't you? A scalie is like a reptile. As opposed to something furry like a wolf, like me. Rodrigo was a dragon. My Draggy." Another puff.

"And you were his Wolfy, I'm guessing?"

"That's right."

"Adorbs. So why did you break up?"

"Probably because he shamed me for abusing a medication I wasn't addicted to."

"Christ."

"Mm-hmm." Another puff.

"And that was before or after Danny?"

"Before. Danny was the best boyfriend anyone could ask for. But I didn't love him. That was when I decided I was done with men. I'm happy with my books, my cat, and baseball. And being happy is the goal, right? So long as you're not harming anyone else."

"I guess that works."

"Well, here we are at my dorm." He extinguished the joint.

They said their good-byes.

9. Torture

Friday, February 8, 2008

"Imagine, just imagine, that someone told you that if you were able to survive one torture session, you'd have a reprieve for several days. You'd welcome the torture in advance, but when it came you'd beg for anything, anything else, and you'd wish that it would go away entirely. Then the relief would come for a few days before it all happened again."

"Is that what you go through, Ox?" I asked.

"Just imagine."

10. Story, Part 1

Tuesday, June 23, 2015

Annie and I sat on my couch. Light filtered in through the living room window, shining onto the back wall, where my liquor cabinets stood.

"I'm having so much trouble with this story," I lamented. "I have some characters, but no plot. And what's the use of a series of unrelated anecdotes? I remember the one time I went to the writing group at the Quincy Library. I read a short story I wrote about me and Randi, and it got eviscerated. They said it was chit-chat. I'll never forget, this one man said, 'Put your characters through hell.' But where is the fire and brimstone here? Why should anyone keep reading?"

"Maybe the plot can be in those anecdotes," Annie said. "What if you explained the hellish story of how your characters ended up where they are? Isn't that a legitimate hell to put them through?"

"Maybe," I said, "but the same thing will happen that always happens. I'll top out at 20,000 words. Nobody wants to publish a novella. I need to get to 40,000, 50,000, ideally 70- or 90,000. I always had trouble in school with word counts. I'm a concise writer. But nobody appreciates concision anymore. They all want prolixity. A hemorrhage of meaningless drivel. That's what people want."

"Maybe your story could even be about *writing* the story. You know, a meta type thing."

"No," I said, "that would be hopelessly pretentious and probably too clever for its own good."

She shrugged. "Well, what will you write about?"

"I have no idea."

11. Goggles Kid

Saturday, August 27, 2011

My roommate was a punk rocker. He was tall and wore an old leather jacket. His name was Hunter. Like me, he was a junior; unlike me, he had been at the college for a couple years already, whereas I had transferred from the salt mines of WCC. I think he saw my mohawk and felt solidarity.

We shook hands and exchanged names. "Well, aren't you cool," he said. "No, seriously, you're cool as hell."

He had a bunch of friends at the college, meaning I had an instant vicarious social life. Often I would be working away at my laptop as they inhabited our room. They mostly played board games and card games, Magic: The Gathering being particularly popular. Sometimes they had D&D sessions. I never joined them, but it was nice to have people around.

Early on, someone (I don't remember any of their names) remarked to Hunter, "Something looks different about you."

"Is it my forehead?" he asked. "The lack of goggles?"

"Yes, that's it!"

"Yeah, I realized I don't need the goggles to be Goggles Kid."

Well, there's our difference, I thought. *He's still a kid. I've been through enough now that I know myself to be a man.*

A week into the semester, I sat alone at my desk, working on an early assignment for pragmatics. The door opened, and Hunter and Annie walked in.

"Red!" squealed Annie, delighted.

"You know each other?" Hunter asked in amazement.

"Oh, yeah," I said. "We're friends. How did you 2 meet?"

"At the fencing club!" said Annie. "We just had our 1st session today."

"Naturally, she's a beginner," he said. "Hey, the 3 of us should do something together."

"I really have to finish this assignment," I said.

"Linguistics, right?" said Annie.

"Yep. And you said you're in the psychology program. What do you want to do with it?"

"I have no idea! Maybe teach little kids someday?"

"Well, anyway," I said, "I'll let you know when I finish this."

They sat on Hunter's bed, talking quietly. I glanced over at 1 point and saw their hands creep toward one another's. I looked back at my laptop. I knew what was coming, and I didn't need to see it.

I finished my assignment: "The Unsaid." I looked over and they were quietly holding hands. "Ah," said Hunter, quickly letting go of Annie's hand. "Done with your assignment?"

"Mm-hmm."

"Well, now that there are 3 of us, how about a round of Icehouse?"

"Icehouse?"

"Yes, I was telling Annie about it. You see, I'm a not-so-secret nerd."

"I had no inkling it was a secret."

"Good. So, there was this dude who wrote a science fiction story, and all the aliens played a game called 'Icehouse.' Everyone who read it wanted to know how to play, but there was no actual game yet. So, this other dude, a friend of his, created one." He pulled out a plastic case and opened it. "These are Icehouse pieces—colored pyramids. Come hither, Red."

The three of us sat cross-legged in a triangle. Hunter explained the rules, which involved the placing of pyramids on the play area. There were upright pyramids and on their side pyramids, called defenders and attackers. There was no clock: players placed their pieces down whenever they wanted. The rules were a tad complicated, and I wasn't very good at it, but it was fun enough.

After a few times, I said, "Well, thanks for the games, but I should get to bed."

"Already, man?"

"Yeah. I don't know if I've mentioned this, but I'm not a whole lot of fun. And I have phonetics tomorrow morning."

"Well, all right."

I took off my pants, feeling no need for modesty in my own room. and turned off my light, then curled into bed. I fell asleep before long.

When I woke up, I heard mumbling and heavy breathing. I stirred. Then I heard a male voice say, "Oh, fuck, Red, I forgot." I pretended to be asleep as Annie embarrassedly got dressed and gathered her things.

B. FUNERALS AVOIDED AND UNAVOIDED

1. The Redmobile, Part 2

Monday February 28, 2022

I went to pick up Annie from her house in Mt. Kisco. She ambled down her staircase and got into my passenger seat. There was a chilly wind and she breathed a deep sigh of relief when she got into my warm car. She had always run cold.

"Shall we?" I said.

I turned out onto the road and began to head north towards Quincy.

"Did you know that *korai* is Japanese for past, and *mirai* is Japanese for future?" she asked in reference to the gen nine mascots. Pokémon Scarlet and Violet had been announced the previous day.

"I had no idea."

We got off the highway and approached the old town. Nothingness gave way to buildings, mostly domiciles, but also a few businesses here and there. "So, this is the old Paciullo house." I pointed.

"Jim lived there?"

"Yes, with his brothers, Rich and Matt, and his parents. Then up here…" I trailed off and climbed the hill. "Up here was the Bonifacio house. This is where my friend Jonathan lived, although everyone called him Bones."

"From the name!"

"Yes, and also he once had his appendix out and couldn't eat for a little while, so he got really skinny. He embraced the nick-name. He usually wore a skull and bones beanie.”

“What happened to him?”

“That, my dear, is a story for another day.” I changed the sub-ject. “Want to see where I went to high school?”

“Sure! I guess all the kids are out for summer break, right?”

“Yep.”

I pulled into the empty parking lot. “Those are called the Four Doors. Every morning, we would all gather there 20 minutes before classes started and… you know, just shoot the shit. And Jim was always there, with his music.”

I stared at the lonely doorway. Suddenly, it hit me like a brick. It was all so… empty. There had been life there! There had been culture! Us! I wondered if the kids even still hung out there. I reflected that even the littlest siblings of all the people I went to school with were long since gone. I sighed and had the thought, *This is why I need to finish my novel.*

“Everything all right?”

“Yes, yes,” I said, snapping back into the present. “Let’s go to my house.” I drove us to the other side of town.

“So, where you’re living now, that’s not anywhere near the house I remember?”

“No. My dad lives nowhere near.” We pulled into my shallow driveway.

“This was my mother’s house,” I said, pausing. “Come on.” We got out of the car and walked into the house. It wasn’t very large. I showed her the living room with the Afghan rug and wood stove, the small TV room, the outdated kitchen, and the short hallway that led to a bathroom and 2 bedrooms, 1 of which of course was vacant. It had been for months now.

“So, all of the furniture, everything, it’s as it was?”

“Yes. When she died, I got a crash course in finance and

homeownership. I was the sole beneficiary of the will, since my parents were divorced, and I'm an only child."

"And did she have any investments?"

"Yes. There was language naming me as a non-spouse beneficiary on her IRA, so I have that, too. How else do you think I live?"

"You could get a job. You've got a degree."

"So few places are hiring. What am I supposed to do, work at Starbucks? You need a graduate degree to even have a fighting chance these days."

"Could you get a graduate degree?"

"What, in linguistics? So I can become a professor or something? Annie, my entire life I've been on the run from academia. I'll do anything to avoid that path."

"Well," she said, "at least you have plenty of time to write."

2. Transition

Wednesday July 6, 2016

I picked up the phone. "Hello?"

"Red?"

"Yes? Who is this?"

"It's Dana. Dana Markson, from college."

"Oh! Hey, how's it going?" I hadn't heard from her in years.

"It's about Hunter."

"Is everything all right?"

"Yeah, it's fine. But I just wanted to let you know that… he's transitioning."

"Transitioning? To what?"

"Red, she's a girl. A woman."

"Oh. I mean, oh! Good for her."

"Red, you're all right with this, right?"

"Of course. I mean, I'm a little surprised. I never had any idea."

"You don't think this could have had anything to do with all her depression? The freaking suicide attempt?"

"Jeez. I never made that connection, I guess. I'm… sorry."

"You should make plans to see her. I'm sure she could use the support."

"I will. So, what is she called now?"

"Randi."

"With an *i*?"

"With an *i*."

"Well, I'll give her a call sometime soon."

"She'd appreciate it."

"Thanks for letting me know about this, Dana."

"Take care, Red."

The line went dead.

3. Wolf

Friday, October 1, 2021

"So, Kev, when did you… awaken?"

"Two and a half years ago, Helen." He sat on his bed. She sat across from him on Jake's bed. Outside there were faint sirens wailing somewhere in the rainy evening.

"What was that like for you?"

"It was profound. An epiphany. I felt myself connected to the ancient steppes, a land before time. I knew I wasn't quite human anymore. But really, what does it mean to be human, anyway?"

"So, you're… both?"

"I mean, of course, I pretend to be totally human. You can't walk digitigrade at school or howl at the moon. But whenever I can, I meditate on wolfiness—lupine meditation. Then I feel myself inhabiting the wolf's body again."

"Interesting," she said. He couldn't tell if she was interested or if she thought he was crazy, like everyone else did. Except Rodrigo.

4. Birthday

Tuesday, June 16, 2009

I had gotten off the late bus at Susan's, as instructed. I walked through the driveway packed with cars and through the backyard, and into the little old house. It looked like it had come right out of the 1930s. There were big windows in the kitchen that let a good amount of light in.

"Have you ever noticed," Bones was saying, "that the word *woodpecker* is a combination of two slang terms for the penis?"

"Imagine how Woody the Woodpecker must feel," Jim's brother Rich said. "They might as well have called him Penis the Penisbird."

A guy stood. He was maybe 5 years older than us. He was tall, with long blond hair and a tuft of a mustache and goatee. "My name is Sven," he said. "I've heard so much about you." He stuck out his hand, and I shook it.

"Yes, this is the friend I was telling you about," said Bones.

"How did you meet again?" I asked.

"My sister, remember? She grew up with him."

"Ah, yes. That's right."

I had no idea what Jim had to do with the whole thing, but it didn't surprise me that he and Rich were there. Socially, Jim was anywhere and everywhere. And Rich was about Sven's age.

"Well, now that you're here, let's get to the main event of the afternoon," said Sven. He went into the kitchen and turned off the light. The room was still bright from the big windows. He took something out of the fridge: a cake, I saw as I glanced. "Let her know that she can come down!"

"Come down!" Bones shouted. A woman appeared from the top of the rickety staircase and made her way down into the living room, and we gathered in the kitchen to greet her.

We all sang in different keys, as always seems to happen when singing "happy birthday." There were 2 candles on the cake: a 5 and a 0. When the cacophony ended, she blew them out, and we all clapped. The smell of the candle smoke wafted towards us.

"Happy birthday, Mom," said Sven.

"Fifty," she said and smiled.

"Do you feel old?" asked her son.

"Not in the least," she said. "My own mother told me she didn't feel old until her youngest turned 40. So, I've got 15 years to go." We cut the cake and ate it. It was a chocolate layered cake.

When we were sated, Sven asked me, "So, do you think you'll audition this year?"

"Audition? For what?"

"Faire, of course."

"The Renaissance Faire? But I'm going to community college this fall."

He shrugged. "Plenty of people juggle school and the Faire."

"I'll think about it."

"Yes, you should consider it," said Susan. "It's been a profound experience for us."

"Why me, though?"

"Bones told me you're a musical guy," said Sven. "There's a lot of music at the Faire. You would get to dress up in period clothing, play the guitar, and sing."

"Hmm."

"Well, think about it," he said.

"All right."

Eventually, I called my father to come get me. It was a Tuesday evening, and the school bus would be coming early the next morning. Susan gave me a big hug. Sven shook my hand again. I imagined Rich would be taking Jim home, and Bones would be staying the night. I said good-bye to my friends and that I would see them tomorrow.

5. Ashes

Monday, December 15, 2014

"Zbigniew," my mother said to me in a shaky voice.

"Yeah?"

"I have some terrible news. I just got a call from Mrs. Byrne. It's about Connor." She began to cry. "He, he…" She choked on her words. Then she took a deep breath. "He's taken his own life." She resumed crying.

I gave her a long hug. I felt like crying myself but resisted. "Connor Byrne," I said to her quietly. "Who would have thought?" After a long while, I let go of her.

Two days later, my mother informed me that Ox's mother wanted me to help scatter his ashes. I walked to the house a few doors down and knocked. A petite woman opened it.

"Mrs. Byrne," I said.

"Please, call me Colleen," she said, then sighed deeply. "You know, you were Connor's best friend. You grew up together. I may not have realized how lonely he was, but you were always there for him."

"What about Jim Paciullo? Or Jonathan Bonifacio? Weren't they there for him?"

"Not always. Come in, come in."

I entered the house. It was warm on that winter's day and smelled nice. She had been boiling water, and she poured it into two tea mugs at the table. I took off my coat, and we sat down. Mine was Earl Grey—my favorite.

"Don't tell anyone else, please, but Connor left a note behind. It said he'd miss you the most."

My heart did a somersault. "Connor…" I said quietly.

"That's why I asked you to come here today." We sipped our

tea in silence. "Well," she said, "shall we?"

We put on our coats, and she grabbed a small ceramic urn from the counter. We walked to the backyard. "Connor, may you find peace at last," she said, scattering the contents of half the urn into the yard. She handed it to me.

"Connor, Ox, buddy…" I shook out the rest.

We stood there for a long time. Then we silently reentered the house. Suddenly, she grabbed me, and we had a lengthy hug. She let go and said, "Thank you, Z."

"I'm so, so sorry," I said. Then I left without another word.

6. Café

Monday, May 24, 2010

One time I was at the Daily Press. There weren't that many customers. I had ordered an almondmilk latte and between sips I played the house guitar. It was a classical guitar with nylon strings, old and not in particularly good condition.

She came up to me. "R.E.M. 'Talk About the Passion.' 1983."

"Yeah!"

"The name's Irene. And I'm craving a cigarette."

She walked in the other direction toward the door and exited the café. I put down the guitar and followed her, carrying my coffee. She rolled a cigarette with a bag of tobacco and a wrapper. As I would soon learn, she was a chimney. She had wavy brown hair and high beams under her tank top. Her armpits were unshaven.

"I've seen you here before," she said as she lit the cig. "Always playing that guitar. You're good, you know."

"I'm okay."

She drew the smoke in, then let it out artistically. "So, you like R.E.M. How about Radiohead?"

"My friend Ox used to like them."

"Come on, get in my car."

"Are we going somewhere?"

"Maybe. For now, just get in my car." She pointed to an old, battered purple station wagon. I obediently climbed into the passenger seat. She got into the driver's seat and rolled down the window. She was still working on that cigarette. She turned the car on, but didn't start it up. She had it set up so that her iPod was connected to the cassette deck.

"This is my favorite album of the moment," she said, and pressed a button on the device. "Airbag" by Radiohead came on.

It was quite loud, but I wouldn't have felt right asking her to turn it down.

"*OK Computer*," I yelled above the music.

She nodded. I had the feeling I might be there a while. A few songs in, she turned it off and said, "I'm bored of that now."

I felt uncomfortable with the whole interaction and said, "I think I'm going to excuse myself back into the café to play the guitar."

"Well, okay," she said. "But I'm sure I'll see you again sometime soon."

"No doubt," I said, scurrying out of the car and back inside. It struck me that she had never asked my name.

7. After School

Friday, June 12, 2009

I lay down quietly on my bed, staring at the band posters on the far wall, the excitement of the week done with. No homework to worry about until Sunday, not that it mattered much. I didn't need to do homework to learn. After a once brutal struggle, my parents had long since given up on policing it.

I didn't know it yet, but this would be one of the last nights I spent with my parents as a family unit. My parents kept their struggle pretty private. My father told me, many years later, that he wanted to wait until I was 18 to divorce my mother to avoid the hassle of a custody battle.

A knock came at my door. "Zbigniew! Dinner!"

I forced myself upright and came to the kitchen. My father was an excellent cook, and tonight, he had roasted some bell peppers filled with couscous, with a salad on the side with homemade lemon tahini dressing. We ate amidst a conversation about the day.

"What's 1 new thing you learned today?" my mother asked, as she often did.

"I learned that the CIA rained down condoms labeled *large* on the communist countries, in order to hamper morale by implying that the capitalists were better endowed."

My father raised his eyebrows but kept chewing with his mouth closed.

Before long I finished my meal. "Great peppers, Dad. May I be excused?"

"Of course, honey," my mother said. "Off to Connor's house?"

"Yep. See you later." I got up and wiped my mouth with a paper napkin. Then I walked down the street a few houses and knocked on the door.

"Hi, Colleen," I said to the woman who answered.

"Oh, hello, sweetie. Connor is upstairs."

I entered and climbed the staircase. There were only 2 doors, a little bathroom that was always funky, and the door to Ox's room. I entered without knocking.

"Hey, Red!" He sat in a big blue beanbag chair and motioned me to sit in the red one opposite. "The red chair for your red hair. That rhymed. Hey, ever gonna do the hawk?"

"If I die without having had a mohawk, my life will have been in vain," I said, and sat down. The walls were all painted black, resulting in a murkiness that could have been described as gloomy, if you didn't know Connor as well as I did.

"So, what'll it be today?" His iPod in its dock and speakers were within arm's reach.

"We already listened to Clan of Xymox on the bus. No more Clan of Xymox."

"Okay, then I'll give you a choice. The Doors or Depeche Mode?"

"That's an odd dichotomy. Hmm. How about Depeche Mode?"

"Great. You know, *Violator* was one of the first albums I ever bought. When I turned 13, I got $50 as a gift, and I went to FYE and bought *A Night at the Opera* by Queen, *Kid A* by Radiohead, and *Violator*."

"I seem to remember that. Excellent choices."

"Today I'm in the mood for some 'Strangelove.'"

"You know, I thought about that song yesterday as I was doing my clothes: Strange wash, strange highs and strange lows. Strange wash, that's how my laundry goes! Strange wash, will you give it to me? Will you take the stain that I give to you, again and again, and will you remove it?"

We both laughed maniacally. "Well, put it on," I said.

"Okay, but we have to listen to the whole album." He was a purist like that. He put on *Music for the Masses*.

I closed my eyes, but unlike having closed eyes when you are alone, when you retreat ever further into your mind, having closed eyes in the company of others is comforting, kind of a warm feeling of gregariousness and platonic affection. We listened to the entire album. I broke the silence by saying, "So what do you want to do after graduation?"

"I confess, I don't know," he said. "I really don't. And you know my mom. She won't pressure me into anything. How about you?"

"I'm going to get my Good Enough Diploma, then go to WCC. Maybe I'll transfer to another college after a couple years."

"Good. You have no business not studying at a college. You're too smart."

I yawned. "Maybe one more, then call it a night?"

"Okay. Your choice this time."

"You have Can on there, right?"

"Yup."

"Then let's do *Tago Mago*."

"You got it."

He put it on, and we listened to the whole album. It ended, and we sat there in our beanbag chairs.

"Red?" he suddenly asked.

"Yeah?"

"Do you think suicide is a selfish act?"

"Well, yeah, in that you really hurt the people you leave behind. What makes you ask?"

"Oh, no reason."

"What about you? What do you think?"

"I think it's selfish of those left behind to think that their suffering at the victim's loss is any greater than the suffering the victim endured at being alive." There was a moment of quiet. Then I wearily got up from the beanbag chair and he followed suit.

"I'll see you Monday morning," I said, "by the Four Doors."

"You got it," he said, and we hugged.

"Good night," I called as I trotted down the stairs. "Good night," I said to Colleen.

"So long, Z," she said.

8. Hospital

Monday, July 2, 2012

I arrived at the hospital with Annie and our other friend Tom Berger. We had to check in at the front desk with our identification. Annie didn't have a driver's license, but they accepted her college ID. We all got wristbands.

We took the elevator up to the psych unit on the 7th floor. There was a strong smell of antiseptic. Doctors and nurses walked by busily with clipboards and stethoscopes. I got the attention of one of them. "We're looking for Hunter Eide?"

"Ah. Follow me," she said, and led us to a small room, then went back to whatever errand she was running.

We walked in. There he was, laying in the bed, with the overhead TV on. "Red," he said weakly. "Annie. Tom. I haven't seen you guys in a while."

"Hunter, I am so, so glad you're okay," I said. "Aren't you glad to be alive?"

"I am," he admitted. "I'm sorry I put you through all that worry."

"Well," Tom said, "if you had died, you never would have gotten to meet my future sons, Ham and Cheese Berger."

Hunter smiled.

"I refuse to believe you really wanted to end your life," Annie said. "We love you too much. Can't you feel our love? We'd be heartbroken if you left us."

"I don't know if I really wanted to end it," he said. "It was just a spur-of-the-moment type of thing. Honestly, I'm glad I don't own a gun, otherwise I'd have been gone a long time ago. It would have been too easy. But after a beer, I stared at my bottle of pills. *What the hell*, I thought."

"Have you really been that depressed?" asked Annie. "We didn't know."

"I have, and I don't know why. Something about this life seems terribly wrong."

"Well, let us know if we can help in any way."

I noticed a bouquet of flowers on the side table. There was a note that said, "For Hunter. Love, Dana."

"Hunter?" I asked.

"Yes?"

"I love you, man. Please feel better."

"Yes, please feel better," echoed Annie.

Tom said nothing.

"Thanks," Hunter said and smiled.

9. After Class

Thursday, August 27, 2009

I sat down in my biology class. I was one of the last students to straggle in, arriving just in time before the session began. I couldn't help but notice her. She was in the seat right behind mine. I didn't dare look back at her once class began, but I couldn't think of anything else. I could barely pay attention to the lecture.

Once class ended, I stood and eagerly turned around to examine her. She was tall and dark, with striking green eyes. We exited the classroom and walked down the hallway in the same direction.

"Hi," I said. "My name is…" I almost said *Red*, but this woman deserved the truth. "Zbigniew."

"How exotic," she said. "But I suppose mine is, too. I'm Aqsa with a *q*."

"I'm glad to meet you. Say, are you doing anything after class?"

"Another class."

"How about before class?"

"Another class."

"You're busy."

"I know. Thursdays are pretty much booked."

"Well, what about any other day?"

"Sorry. I've arranged it so that all my classes are on Thursdays."

I didn't dare request a meetup outside of the context of WCC. We parted ways. Every Thursday in biology class, I'd see her and be transfixed by her beauty, but we never talked again.

10. Funeral

Sunday, December 20, 2020

Unlike Ox's corpse, my mother's was to be interred. It wasn't a big event, and everyone was dressed in black, with black masks, and doing their best to socially distance. It did not stereotypically rain; in fact, it was sunny and unseasonably warm. There was a priest to administer last rites, even though she hadn't attended church in God knows how long.

None of my friends were there, just various adults. I ran into Colleen. "Hey there, Z," she said. "I'm so terribly sorry about Rachel. Even when you know it's coming, it's still hard."

Here is a woman who knows death, I thought. She was intimately familiar with the feeling of losing a loved one, like a string being snipped that was the last thing preventing a precious metal from falling into the eternal abyss.

Speeches were made over the casket before it was lowered into the ground. I didn't know any of the other speakers, but then it came my turn. I tried to project through my mask.

"Rachel McLaughlin Wojcik was a woman. By that, I mean she was full of the stuff that makes you human. She lived with a brightness that infected others, and her mind was always curious. I can't speak for my childhood, as childhood is a time of awareness veiled like a room lit by stained glass. But as an adult, I can say that I am very glad to have known her. She was always courageous in life, even as it eventually led to her demise. So, Mom, it is with that that I say good-bye. Maybe I'll see you again someday. Who knows?" I stepped back and found my place in the front row. Then the casket was lowered.

After the ceremony, several attendees tried to make conversation with me. Nobody could pronounce my name, so after each massacre, I instructed them to call me Z. They told me anecdotes about my mother, some of which I had heard before, some of which I hadn't. The whole thing was extremely tiring for me. I was relieved when everyone dispersed and I could tear off my mask and go back to the house, where I would sleep alone for the first of many, many times.

11. Graduation, Part 1

Friday, June 26, 2009

"I'm so terribly sorry to say this, but you can't go to the graduation," the doctor said. "You have streptococcus. Strep throat. You'll be highly contagious for several days, as the antibiotics begin to work."

"Oh." I was all dressed up, in a suit that featured a blue striped jacket and pants, black dress shoes, a black shirt, and a red tie.

"It's tough for me to have to say that. You look so nice. The only time it was tougher was when a little girl stopped by dressed up as a princess for her school play, and I had to tell her she couldn't do it."

"I was going to go to a friend's house afterward for a party."

He sighed. "The best I can say is you could inform them you're ill, and let them make the decision."

"All right. Thanks." I left the office and drove home. When I got there, I called Jim's house. The machine picked up. "You have reached Jamie, Jocelyn, Rich, Jim, and Matt Paciullo. Please leave a message."

"Hey Jim, it's Red. Listen, I'm sick. I have strep throat. I can't come to your party. I'm very sorry. See you later." I hung up the phone.

I flopped down on my bed. I knew Jim was going off to college somewhere far away in August. I didn't know that I wouldn't see him again for 11 years.

C. LIFE GOES ON

1. The Redmobile, Part 3

Saturday, December 10, 2022

I went to pick up Annie from her house in Mt. Kisco. I met her at her door and kissed her deeply.

"To the Redmobile!" she declared.

We drove to the other side of town to Onegaishimasu, which had just opened its doors to the public.

"That's a weird name for a Japanese restaurant," she said. "Onegaishimasu."

"Why? What's weird about it?"

"That's sort of a formal way of saying 'If You Please.' Like if I were ordering tuna sushi, I might say, 'Maguro sushi o onegaishimasu.' Of course, you can also just say 'kudasai.'"

Abigail was waiting for us. She was still in her red puffy coat and had dark hair in pigtails. I didn't know her, but she immediately struck me as somebody I wouldn't have ever been friends with if she didn't know Annie. We sat across from her.

"Hi," I said. "I'm Red."

"Abigail."

"So, you work with Annie?"

"That's right. I've been teaching the real little ones for a couple years now."

"And how is Stephen?" Annie inquired.

"Very nervous. He's making his first start this coming Thursday night."

"I guess we should get Red here up to speed. Abigail's brother is a pitcher for the Hudson Valley Renegades. He throws a knuckleball!"

"Oh, wow," I said. "As Annie can tell you, I'm a huge Mets fan, and R. A. Dickey is my favorite player of all time." Dickey had been a knuckleballer and was also a huge nerd. I loved that man.

"His, too!" said Abigail. "What a coincidence."

"So, I'm sure you'll be in attendance for that," I said.

The waiter came by. Annie ordered in Japanese to his delight, agedashi tofu and a tuna roll. Abigail ordered (in English) pork dumplings and a soba noodle dish. I ordered (in English) vegetable dumplings, ceviche, and a sweet potato tempura roll.

"The ceviche here is really good," I mentioned as we were waiting for our food. "Really good deal, for all that raw fish."

"Red used to be vegan," Annie explained. "But not anymore."

"No kidding," I said.

"Oh? What made you change your mind?" asked Abigail.

"I made a compromise of sorts," I said. "Between ethics and deprivation. I still don't eat land or sky meat. But I do dairy, eggs, and fish."

"Oh, that's interesting. I eat anything. I don't even think about it."

Too bad, I thought. *Oh well. She would do what she would do.*

Our food came and we quietly ate. I'm a quick eater and finished first.

Once we were all done, Abigail said to Annie, "Oh! I finally beat Eri."

"You need a good flying, fairy, or psychic type for her."

"I have several Pokémon in my party who know flying type moves, and I'm still having trouble with her," I put in. "Even Talonflame."

"You've finished the game, right?" Abigail asked.

"Of course she has," I said.

"I'm mostly hunting shinies now. I want to have an all-shiny team for …"

"For what?"

"Never mind. I don't want to give you any spoilers." To Abigail, she said, "Red hates spoilers."

"Yes, I do."

We were quiet for a while. The waiter came by, and Annie asked for the check in Japanese. It came, and we split it in two: Abigail paid one half, and Annie insisted on covering the other half for the two of us. I always told her I had plenty of money to pay for our meals, but she wouldn't have any of it.

On the way back, she said to me, "I'm glad you got to meet Abigail. After all, she's part of my life. And we're a legitimate couple, right? So, we should be meeting each other's friends, right?"

"If only I had any," I said.

"Come on. You have to have some friends."

"I really wish I did. I haven't even seen Randi in years. And of course, I haven't seen any of my old buddies from back in the day, since, well, back in the day."

We arrived at her house, and I put the car in park. "Annie, you're… all that I've got. Without you, I'd be holed up at my house all day writing novels that will never come to fruition, let alone be published."

She gave me a big hug. "I love you, Red," she said.

"It's mutual," I said, and she got out and disappeared up the stairs.

2. Driving Test

Thursday, October 11, 2007

My driving test was to be in Newburgh. A couple of days prior, my father took me over the river to the test site to gain familiarity with the area. We pulled into the street and found the sign. A police car suddenly pulled up beside us, siren blaring. Police cars always make me nervous. My father rolled down the window as the cop came to our car.

"Sir, this is the DMV test site, correct?" my father asked tentatively.

"Sir, there is a live gunfight going on in this neighborhood!" the cop yelled urgently. "You've got to get out of here!"

So much for that. I came back two days later to take the test. No gunfight this time. The proctor met us there. "Oh," he said forlornly.

"Is everything all right?" my father asked.

"Sir, your registration expired *two years ago*. We can't allow your son to take the test in this vehicle."

He apologized profusely on the way home. He was clearly upset, because at one point we were at a red light behind a number of cars, and after a few moments of the light turning, he leaned on his horn and yelled, "Light's not getting any greener, assholes!"

"I don't think you understand traffic compression and decompression," I said.

I had to book a new appointment on their website. This time it was in Peekskill. My father got the car registered, the day came, and we once again met up with the proctor. He was an African-American man, and he didn't say a word as he got into the passenger seat. I checked my mirrors, then put the car in gear. In lieu of actually looking into said mirrors, I panicked and tried looking over my shoulder to see if anyone was coming. Someone was, but I nonetheless hit the gas.

"Woah, woah, woah!" the proctor shouted, and leaned over to turn the steering wheel back toward the shoulder. I hit the brake. Without another word, he printed out a slip saying I had failed and exited the vehicle. I'm still amazed that I didn't cause a serious accident.

I booked yet another appointment, back in Newburgh this time. The whole thing went very smoothly. I came to a complete stop at every stop sign, and the lady told me my parallel parking was beautiful. For some reason, I'm simply awful at backing up a car, except to parallel park. I had passed!

When I later graduated college, I received an old used Pontiac, red, for my hair. Annie dubbed it the Redmobile.

3. Pandemic

2020

It was March 2020. I said to my father, "Dad, I'm very worried that the coronavirus will jeopardize the baseball season."

"Baseball?" he moaned. "What about my stock portfolio?"

Sure enough, the virus came. Honestly, it was an introvert's dream. My father forbade me from coming over. When I suggested a visit, he yelled at me, "I don't want to end up in a *hospital* on a *ventilator!*"

Annie and I took our chances with one another. If we got sick, we got sick together. My mother was on board with this idea. She knew how much I needed Annie, virus or no virus. We waited for a vaccine, and in the meantime, I worked on my writing. Most of all, I wanted to write something based on my experiences with Jim, Bones and Ox. I had managed several novelettes and novellas, but I couldn't come up with a full-length novel as hard as I tried.

Life was slow and uneventful, but strangely enough, I felt like I was truly living for once, without the distractions of a world that always did its best to pass me by.

On December 14, my mother woke up with a cough that I heard from the next room. She got out of bed eventually and went to make breakfast and I got up, too. She poured her cereal and milk, then a glass of orange juice. She took a sip of it, then froze.

"Zbigniew."

"Yeah?"

"I can't taste this orange juice." She sniffed it. "Or smell it."

"Have you been out lately?"

"Yes. I was at the grocery store yesterday morning."

"Should I take your temperature?" We got a thermometer

from the bathroom medicine cabinet. I put it under her tongue and waited for it to beep. "Ninety-nine point one," I said. "So, a slight fever."

Her cough went away, and she seemed okay. But the next morning, the cough was back and worse, and she complained of muscle and joint pains. She said she was tired, and I took her temperature again. Ninety-nine point three.

In the mail that day was a letter from the government announcing a new free over-the-counter emergency use authorization home antigen test. I rushed to the pharmacy to procure one.

We went through the swabbing process and waited to see if the damning red line would appear on the test. It did.

The next day, her fever was 100, and she had chest pains, so I brought her to the emergency room. After the ordeal of intake, they decided to put her in the ICU.

The whole thing was a whirlwind. Of course, I was tested as well, and I was negative. In order to visit her in person, I would need to wear a snugly fitted mask, plastic gown, face shield and gloves, but I talked to her via FaceTime every day.

Her first full day in the ICU:

Me: Hi, Mom.

Mom: Hi, honey.

Me: How are you feeling today?

Mom: Not so good, I'm afraid.

Me: What's going on?

Mom: My breathing is still a bit difficult. But don't worry. I know I'll be okay, and I'll get out of here soon.

Me: I'm sure you will, too.

Mom: I love you, honey.

Me: I love you, too.

Our daily conversations didn't change much. Then, on the fifth day:

Me: Hi, Mom. How's it going?

Mom: About the same. But I want to tell you something. When the virus came, I had a phone conversation with our lawyer. If something happens to me, you'll be taken care of.

Me: Please, let's not speculate on your death just yet.

Mom: I know, but I wanted you to know.

During the second week, they told me she was deteriorating. I went into the hospital during visiting hours in which they gave me all the protective equipment, and I saw her. She was all hooked up.

"I'm still optimistic I'll get better," she said to me. "I want to live."

"I want you to live, too," I said. I held her hand through my glove.

Three days later, she died.

I called my father for the first time during all of this. For a time afterward, whenever she came up in conversation, he would say, "Well... I guess it's not nice to say bad things about dead people." Eventually, he went back to bashing her.

Places began to open back up. Annie and I got vaccinated. Baseball returned. But my mom was gone.

4. School, Part 1

Friday, September 9, 2011

I sat in the dining hall in front of a plate of quinoa and salad, and a mug of black coffee. To my right was Hunter. Across from me were Annie, Tom, and our friend Sean. The large room was buzzing with noise.

We were all chatting about various topics. The others were all in the fencing club. I had no interest.

"That was kind of a poor choice of words, wasn't it?" remarked Tom. "When Mick was explaining that move, and he said, 'You just want to… *come in their face!*'"

Later during our conversation, Sean said between bites of his chicken, "So Hunter and Annie, you guys… aren't…"

"Nothing happened!" shouted Hunter.

"Sorry."

"'Awk-ward!' hummed Tom quietly.

I decided to mercifully change the subject. "How's your routine coming, Tom?"

"It's coming along nicely," he said, and cleared his throat in preparation. "You know, there's nothing all that *magical* about magic markers. I want to sit down and write a letter to the bastard who invented those. It'll say, 'Dear Sir, I recently purchased one of your so-called "magic" markers… *and I want my money back,* because when I took the cap off, a genie did NOT come out and grant me three wishes!' …Come to think of it, though, maybe *that's* their business plan. You buy one, and after a certain period of owning it… *it disappears!*"

Sean interrupted him. "And then you have to buy another one."

"And then you have to buy another one," finished Tom.

Annie chuckled and clapped her hands together several times.

I was a junior, having gotten my associate's degree at community college, and was studying linguistics, with a concentration in Italian. The major consisted of classes such as pragmatics, syntax and semantics, and phonetics, as well as Italian grammar and translation.

Language had always been a strong suit of mine, and I got along well with my classmates and professors. Hunter and his friends kept me company in my dorm room. And although Annie no longer visited my room after the incident with Hunter, we continued to stay in touch and get coffee sometimes. She was very excited about the upcoming Pokémon games.

One day we were at Starbucks. "I'm sorry you and Hunter didn't work out," I said.

"It's okay. You know, I still see him often."

"Oh? That's cool."

"Not always."

"Why? What's up?"

She sighed. "I'm tired of him calling me up every time he has a panic attack. I mean, I try to be helpful. I really do. But it's getting to be a bit much."

"Panic attacks? I haven't noticed those."

"Yeah. He's very good at hiding them from people."

"Do you think I should talk to him?"

"That might be a good idea. Like I said, it's getting to be a bit much for me to handle."

That evening, after everyone had left our room, and my roommate and I were lying in our beds, I said, "Hey, Hunter?"

"Yeah?"

"Is everything all right?"

"Why wouldn't everything be all right?"

"I don't know. Annie mentioned to me that you might be having some trouble."

"Oh."

"Well, if you ever need an ear, I'm here."

"Thanks."

The semester went on and eventually ended. I went home and didn't see any of my friends. Irene, of course, was long gone, living her new life in New Mexico. Bones never wanted to see me again. Ox and I had drifted apart since I left for the college. And Jim was a mystery. I wondered whether I'd ever see him again, either.

The spring semester began. Hunter seemed more reserved than before. Our room was empty more of the time.

Then one day a couple weeks in I was working at my desk, and Hunter and Annie crashed into the room. Hunter was crying. "I just— I just—" he blubbered.

"There, there," Annie said. "Why don't you sit down?" She guided him to his bed, and he sat.

He breathed. "I'm tired of this place. I've tried majoring in chemistry. I've tried majoring in math. I've done everything, and I'm not going anywhere. I didn't want to come here. I wanted to live in the city and have a band."

"Well, what if we could do something musical here?" Annie said. "Organize a show? Red plays guitar, too." "I know," he said. He seemed to be calming down. "Okay."

"Does that sound like a good idea?" she said.

"Okay."

Annie and I started planning an acoustic punk show, featuring me, Hunter (billed as Vodka Enema, his hypothetical band) and their friend Guillermo, from the fencing club. It would take place in the mail tunnel the following Saturday night. I created colorful fliers and we posted them around campus, and she used her considerable word-of-mouth power.

The time came. I lugged my guitar out of my closet; I had

scarcely touched the thing in my time at the college. Hunter and I trudged down to the mail tunnel that was accessible from behind the mailroom. There were all sorts of urban legends regarding the original purpose of these tunnels and why they were there, but no one seemed to know for sure.

We were met there by about 10 people, including Annie, Tom, and Sean, as well as others I didn't recognize, but who seemed to be part of the general social circle. We waited to see if anyone else would straggle in, and a couple more people showed up.

We had decided that Guillermo should go first. He announced himself as a Chicano punk and started off with a tune called "El Baile del Chupacabras," followed by "Me Gusta el Pan." The guy was a wizard with his instrument, blending a punk sound with Spanish inflections. He played for about 20 minutes and got a rousing ovation.

"Want me to go next?" Hunter asked.

"Nah, man, you're the headliner. I'm just a warm-up act."

I took my guitar out. "Need a pick?" he asked.

"Nope, I play bareback."

He smirked.

I stood up front of everyone and they quieted down. "Just so you guys are aware, I know I used to have a mohawk, but my music isn't particularly punk. It's more prog. Anyhow, this is an instrumental called 'Il Rossotino,' which is something a teacher used to call me."

I played the song and stumbled a few times but got through it. I remembered the advice someone had once given me that when something like that happens as a musician, you're a lot more likely to notice than anyone else. Then I said, "Anyone here a Neil Young fan?" Silence. "Well, here's a Neil Young medley." I went into a rendition of "My My, Hey Hey" followed by "Rockin' in the Free World." It was well received. After a little while, I decided I had played long enough. "And now, ladies and gentlemen, Vodka Enema!" We all clapped for my friend.

His music was classic punk in its sound, simple but effective. His first song was called "Intercourse, Pennsylvania." His entire set used about 3 different chords, but hey, sometimes that's all that's needed. We all seemed to enjoy his music, and the cross-legged audience applauded.

That was the end of the show. By all accounts, it had been a success. I was glad for Hunter. An artist with no outlet for his art is like a creature beneath the skin, trying desperately to escape to find air to breathe.

A week later, I came back from class to a half-empty dorm room. I was subsequently informed by resident services that Hunter had dropped out. There was the possibility I might be assigned another roommate, but until that happened, I'd be on my own.

5. The Summer of Irene

Sunday, May 30, 2010

I was at the Daily Press, playing the house guitar in between sips of my almond milk latte, taking care not to spill the hot foam over the lip of my mug. I was working on an original tune called "Flower Moon."

"You should take singing lessons," she said, sitting across from me. "Or get a vocalist." It was Irene from Monday. I was offended but didn't tell her so. Instead, I said, "My name is Red."

"Ah, because of your dyed hair."

"Yeah."

"How old are you?"

"Care to hazard a guess?"

She looked me over. "25?"

"Believe it or not, I'm 19. How old are you?"

"Care to hazard a guess?"

I looked her over. "25?"

"Believe it or not, I'm 31."

"So, you're something of a geezer, I guess," I said playfully.

"And you're something of a baby." Her tone was serious and somewhat condescending. "It's such a beautiful day. Let's go outside. Take your coffee."

I put away the guitar and followed her outside into the early May afternoon, coffee in tow. The sun was beating down on the cracked parking lot asphalt. There was a smell in the air like hope.

Irene rolled a cigarette. "So, what's your deal?" she asked as she smoked it.

"Well, I just finished my first year at WCC. I plan to get my associate's next spring and then transfer somewhere else."

"What do you want to study?"

"Linguistics. Hey, want to hear a linguistics joke I came up with the other day?"

"Go right ahead."

I cleared my throat. "Yo momma's so dumb, she thinks the TV distinction is whether to watch *The Bachelorette* or *Desperate Housewives*!"

She stared at me.

"Never mind," I said meekly.

"I went to college a long time ago."

"Oh, when did you graduate?"

"I didn't. I was going to be a respiratory therapist." She sighed. "But that's all in the past now."

"So how do you spend your time?"

"I write poetry."

"That's pretty neat. I'm more of a prose writer. I'm working on what I hope will become a novel." I thought she might ask what it was about, but she didn't.

We became fast friends. I invited her over to my mom's house and she liked her. She wouldn't tell me where she lived; I assumed it was with her folks. We mostly hung out at the café. Early on in our friendship, she asked me what my hobbies were, and I mentioned I liked billiards. She invited me to the pool hall in town.

"How long have you played?" I asked.

"Oh, I've been playing in bars forever. You?"

"Since I can remember. My grandpa in Pennsylvania had a table in his basement."

I set up the balls in the rack and removed it. "Mind if I break?" I asked.

"Go ahead."

I broke, and the balls separated nicely; the 5 found its way to the corner. Then I sunk the 3 before missing my shot on the 7.

She surveyed the table, then sidled up to the cue ball. Without any preparation whatsoever, she attempted to shoot the ball and didn't get a solid strike: the ball lamely rolled across the table where it quietly collided with the 8. She groaned in frustration. That was when I realized I'd have to go easy on her. Even though I let her win, she couldn't beat me.

After 3 rounds she said, "I don't think I want to play any more pool. I'm going to drop you off at your house and go home."

This exact routine took place several times.

Once we were chatting on the phone. She asked how I was. I mentioned that New York had lost to Miami, following it up with, "But I know you don't really care about baseball."

"Yeah," she said, "I really don't," and laughed. She was imperfect, but I hadn't had a friend as close as her since Ox and I were younger. Every other day, she wanted to hang out. Often, we sat in her car and listened to music.

One day in late July she announced, "I'm moving to New Mexico, and I want you to come with me."

"New Mexico? What's there?"

"They call it the Land of Enchantment. I want to live in the desert. Somewhere far away. Away from all this never-ending series of dead-end small towns."

"I get that, and it sounds romantic and all, but I can't come with you. I need to stay here to finish college."

"Is it really that important to you?"

"Yes. It is."

A couple weeks later, she came by with her silver sedan loaded up with stuff, to say good-bye. In her black tank top, she approached me and gave me a long hug. We stood there for a few moments, then I hugged her again. "I know," she said. "We won't see each other again for a really long time." Then she left.

     INSTANT REPLAYS OF THE EXODUS

6. Bushwick

Sunday, July 5, 2015

I drove to the train station, traveled down into the city, boarded the 4 at Grand Central, transferred to the L, got off at Myrtle-Wyckoff and then walked a few blocks until I reached the little brunch place. I was a little nervous, since I hadn't seen her since she was Hunter. I entered, and she sat at a table. When she saw me, she got up.

"Red," she said.

"Randi," I said, and we had a good hug. She was wearing a skirt and a blouse and had bright red lipstick on. Other than that, she looked more or less the same. Tall, with a shock of dirty blonde hair. This was still my friend, no question about it.

"So here you are in the city," I said.

"I am."

"Do you have a band?" I felt bad that we had fallen so far out of touch, I didn't even know.

"I do!"

"Vodka Enema?"

"Actually, we're called The Third Rail Pissers. I play guitar and sing, and we've got a bassist and a drummer."

"Sounds… *electrifying.*" We both chuckled. It was good to see her again.

"What about you?"

"Well, I graduated from the college. To be honest, I haven't really done anything with the degree. The job market is so shitty."

"Tell me about it. I managed to snag some hours at Trader Joe's. And that's just enough to live where I live, and trust me, you do *not* want to see my apartment."

"But you're happy?"

"I'm happy."

"I'd ask you if you were dating anyone, but that would just recall Tom Berger. Remember?"

"'I've been single for a while,'" remembered Randi. "'I tried dating a girl who worked for a toothbrush factory, but she only gave me Oral-B.'" We both chuckled again.

"I don't know what happened to that guy," I said." I've lost track of most everyone."

"Are you still in touch with Annie?"

"Well, as a matter of fact… we're dating."

Randi looked at me in amazement. "You and Annie? Hey, congrats, man!"

"Thanks. We've got a good thing going."

"Well, I've got a girlfriend too. Her name is Kim. Actually, she's the bassist in my band."

"Bassist Kim. Like in the Pixies."

"Yeah! Funny coincidence."

The waitress came, and I ordered two poached eggs. Randi ordered a stack of pancakes.

"Not vegan anymore, huh?" she said.

"I'm afraid not. I'm pescatarian."

"That's fish?"

"Yeah."

Her voice was still masculine. I didn't know much about gender transition, but it was my understanding that that was something that could get fixed with hormones or surgery. "I'm in a good place, Red," she said. "I'm on estrogen and anti-androgen."

"What's that second one?"

"It's a T-blocker. Blocks testosterone."

"Well, I'm so glad you're doing this. Authenticity is key."

"You've got to be yourself. Speaking of which, I don't know

how you'll react to this, but I have to say something: Jesus Christ is the answer."

"Oh."

"You may not have any reaction to it at all, but He died for you and loves you."

"Thanks." I didn't know what else to say. Our food came and at a good moment, too. We ate quietly. When the bill came, I insisted on paying it.

We walked out onto the sidewalk. "It was really good to see you, Red."

"It was great seeing you too, Randi." She hugged me, and I walked back toward the train.

7. Faire

Friday, June 19, 2009

I got off the late bus at Susan's house after chess club Friday and walked in. Bones hadn't been in school all day, but Sven was there.

"Where's Bones?" I asked Sven.

"Jonathan and Kayla's grandmother passed away. They're in Florida."

"Does that mean there's a spot in the car for me to come to Faire auditions tomorrow?"

"Looks like it."

"Oh, good."

The next day, they came to pick me up at my house. Susan drove, Rich was in the passenger seat, and Sven and I were in the back.

We drove the hour to the audition site. The driver and the other 2 passengers had a lively conversation about the Renaissance Faire in years past, including the "flood year." Finally, we arrived. We parked and walked across a field to a large barn. There were a great number of people in the building. My traveling companions were very sociable, but I felt out of place. I had to wait a long time for my audition.

Finally, I was called in front of a panel of 3 men.

"Do you ever think of yourself as actually dead…" I began. It was a monologue from *Rosencrantz and Guildenstern Are Dead.*

When I finished, one of the men said, "I'm impressed. We thought it would be like pulling teeth getting words out of you. Thank you for your audition."

Eventually it was time to go home. By the time we got back to Susan's house, it was very late.

"You can stay here for the night, you know," said Sven. I agreed and was shown a small room with a bed in it. I fell asleep immediately.

When I woke Sunday morning, my pants were around my ankles. I was very confused. Had I pulled them down prior to conking out? Or had something more sinister occurred?

I got dressed and went into the kitchen.

"Good morning," Sven said.

"Good morning," I said tentatively.

"Sleep well?"

I couldn't gauge if there were any undertones to this query. "I don't think I'm going to do the Faire," I said.

"Oh, bummer," said Sven. "How come?"

"I just don't," I said. "I want to focus on school."

"Well, if you say so."

"I'd like to go home."

"I can drive you home," said Susan.

On the way home, she said to me, "Don't mind my son. He's a bit of a wild card."

I didn't dare ask her what might have happened the previous night. When we arrived at my house, she said, "I'm sure I haven't seen the last of you, kiddo."

"No doubt. Thanks for the ride."

I would see her again for sure. But I'd end up wishing I'd never met her in the first place.

8. School, Part 2

Saturday, May 4, 2013

"So what's new with you?" Annie asked.

"Well, I think tonight's game is going to be postponed, due to the rain," I said. "Although I know you don't really follow sports,"

"No, but I know you're passionate about your baseball, and I respect that," she said.

"You know something? Remember that friend of mine Irene that I mentioned once? You're such a better friend to me than she ever was. Did you know that she once laughed in my face because I like the Mets?"

"That's not cool."

I sipped my almond milk latte. These coffee dates with Annie were all that kept me going at times. I spent most of the rest of my free time shooting pool all by myself at the student center, an enormous and lonely facility. After a spring semester that had left me roommate-less after the departure of Hunter, I lived in an apartment-style dorm my senior year with Joshua and Saketh. Joshua was nice, but Saketh was snarky. I didn't interact with them much.

My graduation was one of the most important days of my life. Of course, I was graduating college, but more important was that I asked Annie out. She came to the graduation and sat with my mom's side of the family. My dad had come on his own and sat separately. I had instructed them all not to cheer when my name was read. I graduated summa cum laude.

Following the ceremony, my dad hugged me and told me how proud he was of me, then left.

There was to be a meal at my mom's house afterward. One of

my aunts had come to visit, and Annie joined us as well. At one quiet moment before dinner, as everyone was just visiting, I asked Annie if she'd come to my room.

"Annie," I said. "You're maybe the best friend I've ever had. But I have an inkling there's something more significant going on between us."

"I know," she said. "I've known for a very long time, but I was too nervous to say anything."

"I'm nervous, too. So, I guess I'll just say it." I sighed. "Would you go out with me?"

"Of course, Red!"

I smiled so wide I felt my mouth would creep off my face. I felt like crying. We embraced. Then I kissed her for the first time.

"There's something you should know about me. My name isn't Red Parsons."

"I know. You said your real name is unusual and starts with a letter near the end of the alphabet."

"Right. And you can still call me Red."

"Of course I will. But I'm curious now… what's your real name?"

"Zbigniew."

9. Last Words

Sunday, December 28, 2014

I sat alone in my room. Ox had been dead for a few weeks. Colleen had said to me that I'd always been there for him. I wanted to take comfort in that belief. But the truth was I'd abandoned him, just as everyone else had. I'd gone off to college after high school, and I was sure that's what he wanted for me: He had been kind enough to say that I was too smart not to go.

At that point, though, our lives diverged. I met other people like Annie and even Irene for a little while. He lived in his own dark little world that gradually spiraled downward.

I had seen him two days before he died. I was at the café in town, sipping an almond milk latte. He walked in and sat next to me without a word and took off his coat.

"Hey there," I said.

"Hi, Zbigniew," he said. He didn't usually call me that anymore.

"What have you been up to lately?"

"It's too bad you don't come over anymore," he said, not answering my question.

"Oh." I felt guilty.

"Yes, no one seems to come over anymore. All this time we have!" He seemed different somehow. He had always been reserved, but the best way I could put it was now he acted like a ghost.

"What have you been listening to?" I asked.

"Nothing new. Depeche Mode. Joy Division, lots of Joy Division. Ian Curtis died very young, you know."

"Yeah, I know."

"Maybe he saw no way forward. When the car is barreling

toward the cliff, there's no use trying to brake if the brakes don't work, the car is moving very fast, and the cliff is approaching."

"Are you okay, Connor?"

He stared at me for several seconds. Then he said, "The world will be just fine, even when its angels have all gone away." He got up, put his coat on, and left.

I probably should've done something. At least called his mom. In the end, I was left wondering if those had been his last words: *The world will be just fine, even when its angels have all gone away.* If that was it, if he had never said anything to anyone again, then what fucking beautiful last words, sad though they were. He may have been gone, but the world still had the opportunity to heal itself.

PART TWO: KEVIN

D. AWAKENINGS

1. Ganja, Part 1

Friday, January 3, 2020

I met Jim Paciullo a few times. My sister's boyfriend had been friends with him a long time ago, but I was good friends with his younger brother Matt from NYU, and I ran into him occasionally at their house.

Once I was over there, hanging out in Matt's room. We were on winter break, following the first semester of our sophomore year. His ceiling was entirely covered with CDs, shiny side down. It made a nice effect when his lamp hit it. It was my first time there.

"So…" I said.

"Yeah?"

"We've been friends for a little while now."

"We have."

"Then I guess I should let you know that I'm gay."

Matt laughed. "I know, dude. Trust me, it doesn't matter to me."

I breathed out. "Good. That's a bit of a relief."

"You really thought I'd care?"

"I don't know."

"So… you got a boyfriend?"

"Sort of, but he lives in Yankton."

"Yankton? Where's that?"

"South Dakota."

"How the hell do you have a boyfriend in South Dakota?"

"We met online."

"Ohhh. So, you haven't met in person."

"Not yet. I really want to visit. I'm thinking of flying out there next spring break."

"He won't come to New York?"

"He wants me to visit."

"What's his name, anyway?"

"Matthew."

"And how old is he?"

"26."

"Ooh. So, you're into older men."

"It always seems to work out that way."

There was a knock at the door. "It's Jim," he said.

"Open up," called Matt.

Jim opened the door and poked his head in. "You want to…" He made a circle with his thumb and index finger and lifted them to his mouth and breathed in.

"Sure. Come on, Kev."

He stood up from his bed and I got up from my cross-legged position on the floor. We put on our coats at Matt's suggestion: It would be cold in the garage. We followed Jim, and he shut the inside door.

"You ever done this?" asked Jim.

"You mean… smoke marijuana? Is that what we're doing?"

He laughed. "Yeah, we're smoking pot. Doobie. Ganja."

"No, I haven't."

"Well, you're in college now, so it'll happen eventually. Good to have a safe space to get started."

"Do I need to pay?"

Jim cracked up. "Marijuana is a generous drug. You'll learn that, too." He produced from his pocket a small bowl and a little plastic box with the drug in it. He packed in the green buds and then took out a lighter from the other pocket. He lit the bowl and took a toke, measuring his breath beautifully. Then he passed the paraphernalia to me. I lit the bowl and nervously breathed in and immediately had a horrible coughing fit. Jim and Matt both laughed.

"Slowly," said Matt. "Try again."

That time I breathed in slowly, held it in for a few beats as Jim just had, and exhaled.

"Excellent," said Jim.

I passed everything to Matt. It was a small bowl, so it only went around twice.

"And thus you are christened," said Jim. "Let's go inside."

I staggered into Matt's room and lay on the ground. I was totally high, brain and body. I don't remember anything else that happened that night. I woke up the next morning in the fetal position on Matt's floor.

"Awake?" he asked, standing over me.

"I think so." I got up.

"Man, you're funny when you're stoned. Do you know what you kept saying before you fell asleep last night?"

"I have no idea."

"You kept saying," he laughed, "'With all due respect, Officer, my underpants are on backwards.'"

"Seriously?" I was embarrassed but snorted anyway.

"Yeah."

"I think I should go home now."

"You might want this." He handed me a box of white Tic-Tacs. "Or I don't know, maybe your folks don't care."

"Probably best that my mom doesn't know. Annie might not care, but she lives on her own now. And my dad lives in California, remember?"

"I remember."

I called my mom to come pick me up and ate a bunch of
Tic-Tacs as I waited. Matt and I would reconvene the following
week in the city.

    INSTANT REPLAYS OF THE EXODUS

2. Red

Saturday, August 27, 2011

We arrived at the college to help Annie move into her room. It was a sultry late August day. Annie, my mom, our dog and I were walking across campus, and suddenly we spotted this hot guy with a red mohawk.

She shouted she loved his hair and ran up to him. I didn't catch any of their conversation, but I saw them with their phones out, presumably exchanging numbers. Then she rejoined us. "That guy is called Red!"

"Real creative," I muttered.

"Is that his real name?" asked my mom.

"I don't think so," said Annie.

I had just hit puberty, and that night I masturbated to him.

A few weeks earlier, I had run into Carissa at the supermarket, of all places. "Did you get my email?" I asked tentatively.

"Yes, and my eyes went as wide as dinner plates. Then they went back to normal, and I said, 'Oh, okay.'" She was the first person I'd ever come out to.

3. Matthew

Monday, March 17, 2019

I was waiting at Minneapolis-Saint Paul International Airport. I've always found big airports to be very exciting places, because everyone is going somewhere. It's kind of like driving on an Interstate highway, only nobody is flying to the supermarket or church. My layover was 2 hours. Then I would fly to Sioux Falls, take the bus to Vermillion, SD, then a taxi to Matthew's house. I'd been invited for 3 nights.

I bode my time, sitting at the terminal. Of course, it was all crazy. I was spending all the money I had. I had known Matthew online since two Augusts ago. I had met up with guys before that I'd met online, but this was something entirely different. He was 26, and my own big sister was only 25.

I boarded the plane. The flight was 1 hour and 11 minutes. Then the bus. Then the taxi. Then I arrived at his door. I nervously rang the doorbell.

He opened the door and enthusiastically spread his arms out. I stepped in and gave him a hug. He looked just like in his photos: tall, very long, wavy brown hair, glasses.

"I'm getting some dinner ready," he said. "You must be hungry."

He retreated to the kitchen. I said, "I could use a drink of water. Is the tap water okay?"

He turned to me and said, "As a loyal citizen, I trust the government not to poison me."

Soon dinner was ready: seared scallops and baby spinach with spiced pomegranate glaze. It was as good as you would expect from a culinary school graduate. We ate silently.

After he did the dishes, refusing my offer to assist, I said,

"You know, you promised me a back rub. I'm a bit sore from all that travel."

He smiled. We went into his bedroom, and I lay down. He rubbed my back, but his hands quickly wandered southward. I turned in surprise to look at him. "If you think you're ready," he said.

"I'd really just like a massage for now," I said.

"Okay," he said quickly.

The next morning, we had sex. "Was I your first?" he asked.

"I'm afraid not."

"Oh. That's too bad."

He got a French press ready, grinding the beans coarsely, and boiling water. When the water was ready, he poured it in and let it steep for five minutes. Then he poured himself a mug and sat down across from me at the little table. I looked at him expectantly, but he didn't meet my gaze. Finally, I said, "May I have a mug?"

"Sure," he said, and went to pour me one.

"I had to ask?"

He frowned. "I figure if someone wants something, they'll ask for it."

That afternoon, he worked at his computer. He was busy writing his master's thesis for women's studies. To this day, I don't recall what it was about. He started coughing at one point.

"Are you okay?" I asked.

"I think so."

That evening, he made baby beet and flank steak salad dijon. He didn't seem totally well, though.

"I feel like homemade shit," he mumbled after dinner.

"Is there anything I can do?" I asked.

"No, I just need to sleep it off. Best to stay away from me so you don't get it, too."

I sat at the table with my computer and browsed the web. I felt it would be unfaithful to Matthew to look at porn, so I avoided it. By the evening, he still hadn't left the bed. "Aren't you hungry?" I asked.

"No."

"I am."

"My wallet is on the dresser. Go get something from McDonald's." I walked down the block and got myself 3 orders of fries.

The next morning, he seemed a bit better. He got out of bed, at least. But the day had come for me to leave. "I'll drive you to Vermillion," he said. I got my things together and got in his car.

"Kevin, I'm sorry we weren't more intimate. Nothing makes me less horny than being sick." We got to the bus stop. He put the car in park and I leaned over and kissed him on the lips. Then I got my stuff, and he left.

After that, we didn't really talk online as much. Eventually, we barely talked at all. At one point, Matt asked me if we were still dating. I said no.

4. Carissa

Wednesday, July 27, 2011

Carissa had joined the academic triathlon team in the 7th grade. I have to admit that her personality was perfect for it: smart, creative, and outgoing.

For my birthday that year, she got me a black bracelet adorned with shiny silver spikes. I felt right wearing it. I gradually wore more black clothing to go with it.

Once that summer, she was at my house. "I'll help you with your hair," she said mischievously, and pulled a bottle of hairspray out of her bag. It had a "5" on it, indicating maximum hold. "Let's go to the bathroom," she suggested.

"We're not cutting my hair at all, are we?" I asked nervously.

"Nope, just styling it a bit. Now hand me that comb."

I obeyed. My hair was medium length, but parted in the middle so that it went over my ears.

She immediately combed the entire right half of my hair straight down, so it went over my eye. "I can't see out of my right eye," I said.

"Don't worry. You've got 2 eyes to see with."

Then she lifted the left side of my hair skyward and attacked it with hairspray. She repeatedly combed and pulled and sprayed until it was firmly upright. "Look in the mirror. You look like a rock star."

I did. "I like it." I smiled.

"We must document this. In your bedroom."

I obeyed. She had me stand in front of an empty patch on one of my walls, took out her phone, and snapped pictures. Then she stared at me. "Kev."

"Yes?"

She suddenly got on her knees and put her hand on my thigh, which then crept northward.

"Carissa, no," I said. She ignored my protest. I felt myself getting hard despite myself. "No!" I shouted. She stopped and reluctantly got to her feet.

By the 8th grade, she became even more of a social butterfly, and I dropped several ranks on her friendship list. By high school, we didn't talk at all.

Many years later, I was at the mall with my mom, and I heard my name. I looked and saw someone I didn't recognize. "Kev!" she said again. "Carissa? Remember?"

"Oh yeah," I said. "How are you?"

"I'm good. I'm a manager here at Old Navy. I'm the youngest one, the baby manager. How about you?"

"I'm studying anthropology at NYU."

"Well, nice to see you."

"You, too." The whole thing was somewhat awkward, and my mom and I continued on our merry way.

Sometimes I wish I'd just let her give me the blowjob, or the hand job, or whatever she'd planned.

5. Young Millionaire

Friday, March 2, 2012

"Are you really a millionaire?" I asked on the phone.

Paul laughed. "Yes, I am. Everyone asks that. It all depends on what kind of lifestyle you want to have. I didn't want to go to school to become a lawyer or a doctor, so I went into business."

Eventually, he told me he would send me an iPod as a gift. I gave him my address. It never came, and I told him.

"Yeah, they said it needed to be signed for, and no one was home."

The next day, he said, "Do you really live at," and then my address, "?"

"Of course," I said.

"Really? I'll bet you gave me a fake address."

"No, that's my real address—I swear!"

"Yeah, right."

And that was that.

6. Oils

Thursday, June 28, 2012

I deliberately lost another round of poker. I took off my underpants, which were my last remaining piece of clothing.

He wouldn't look. He was turned away, with a blanket covering his otherwise bare chest.

Oils, he had said.

The next day, I returned to try to find the Velvet Underground CD I had left there. I opened the unlocked door, and no one was home. There was the CD on the table. *Whew.* If I had lost it, my mom would've been pissed.

7. Story, Part 2

Sunday, April 16, 2017

Red and Annie sat on Red's couch. He had a thin laptop sitting on the chipped mahogany coffee table.

"None of this is the least bit original," he said to her. "It's all little bits and pieces of things that have happened to me in my own life. And imagine if someone read it who knew me well. They'd know immediately, for example, 'Hey, that guy in the story, Clayton, that's really Ronny.' I need some sort of actual plot."

"I'm sure you can think of something."

"I sure hope so."

8. Goths and Furries

Friday, May 24, 2019

Long before I met my best friend Helen, I was friends with a girl named Jess. This was when I was in my first year in the city.

Her roommate must have been out for the night because I was lying on the bed opposite hers. The walls needed repainting and the bathroom door stuck, but you couldn't really expect too much more from an NYU dorm. We had both had a few beers and were listening to music. She had great taste in music: She had just introduced me to "Is This the Life?" by Cardiacs.

"You're studying anthropology, right?" she said, pausing her playlist. "Maybe you can write your thesis on goths and furries."

"What?" I laughed.

"Well, that falls under the realm of anthropology, right?"

"Goths and furries?"

"They're not so different, you know. Goths like to pretend to be vampires, furries like to pretend to be animals. Looks like you're already a goth." I looked at my black outfit and spiky bracelet. I couldn't argue. "I'll take you to Anthrocon next month. It's a furry convention in Pittsburgh."

"But I don't think I'm a furry."

"Well, I'm one. And we'll see about you. What about that necklace you're wearing?"

I glanced down again. It was a wolf.

"Do you feel an affinity for wolves?"

"Well, yes…"

"Well, there you go. Come with me to the convention. We'll see about you."

The end of June came, and we boarded a crowded bus to Pittsburgh. It was something entirely new to me. Many of the passengers were already decked out in full animal suits. Jess struck up a conversation with a guy sitting across from us. His *fursona* was a wolf, hers was a tiger. She introduced us: His name was Luis. Mine was Kev.

"What's your fursona?" asked Luis.

"I… don't really have one," I stammered.

"Yet," said Jess.

"Well, are there any animals you like in particular? Wolves are popular. I see you're wearing a wolf necklace. I'm a wolf myself."

"Sure," I said.

"All right, so now you need a name. I can draw you, too," he said, pulling out his tablet and stylus.

"What are your names? I mean, your furry names?"

"Sabine," Jess said.

"And I'm Wolfgang Fuzz. What do you want to be called?"

I thought. Wolves were lupine. "Loopy," I said. It sounded silly.

"Excellent!" Luis said. "I'll start drawing you. I can picture you already." He got to work on his tablet.

Somewhere around Scranton he addressed me. "Kev! Look what I've come up with." He showed me. It was a wolf character, dressed in black with a spiky bracelet, shown from the front and in profile.

"It's adorable," I had to admit.

"Great! So now you can introduce yourself as Kev, also known as Loopy."

"So what should I call you?"

"Whatever you want. Wolfgang, Luis, whatever."

"So… Wolfgang. Where are you from?"

"I'm from Boston, and you?"

"I'm from Mt. Kisco, New York. Jess is from Brooklyn."

"And you met in the city?"

"We go to NYU," I said.

"Nice, nice. I study at MIT myself."

"Wow, impressive."

"Who says you can't be into both math and furries?" We were quiet for a while. Then somewhere along I-80 Jess asked him if he was staying at the Westin. He was. So were we.

I asked him to email me the sketches of my new fursona. Now I would have them on my phone in case anyone asked.

The whole thing was overwhelming: the registration, people in fursuits everywhere. On Saturday, they had the parade down 10th Street: literally the entire street in the middle of Pittsburgh cordoned off for it. There were also all sorts of activities at the hotel.

Throughout that evening, back indoors, I noticed a person (a guy?) in what appeared to be a leopard suit, hanging around close to me. Finally, he approached me and said, "Kitty wants a snug?"

I was very confused, but managed to get out, "I'm a wolf. Loopy the Wolf." It still sounded silly to me. He made a motion in the air as if to dismiss what I had just said, then stood there. I wasn't sure what he wanted, so I said tentatively, "Should we… go back to my room?" He nodded.

We got there, and Jess wasn't there. He lay on the bed she and I were sharing. Again, I didn't quite know what to do, so I lay next to him. Then he took the head off his fursuit, and I finally got a look at him. He had medium-length hair and a five o' clock shadow. I had to guess he was at least 5 years older than I was, maybe much more.

Suddenly, he kissed me all over the neck. The whole thing was absurd, with him still in the majority of his suit. I turned my head away, but he kept kissing me on the ear and neck. Finally, he whispered aggressively, "Just kiss me," but I wouldn't.

I felt like I should maybe do something, anything, to reciprocate, but the fursuit clearly precluded that possibility. Not for the first time in my life, I felt myself getting physically aroused despite myself. I suddenly remembered Carissa.

Eventually, I had no choice but to finish by my own hand. He stopped the assault, picked up a sock lying on the floor, and handed it to me, saying, "You get a sock." I cleaned myself up.

"What's your name, anyway?" I asked.

He looked at me with an inscrutable expression, then said, "Kilometers. Get it? Like Miles, only..." Then he stopped and put his head back on. He paused by the door, then left.

The next morning, I noticed on the schedule a panel called "Therians and Otherkin." It sounded interesting, so I showed up, figuring I had some time before we had to board the bus back to New York.

It wasn't particularly well attended, but after everyone got settled, 1 of the 3 women behind the table said, "What does it mean to be human, anyway? What if there's something more? Or maybe not more, but less, even?"

I was intrigued. She used the word *therian.*

"A lot of us like to pretend to be animals," she went on. "But for therians, such as my colleagues and me, it's possible to be that animal as well. We experience what are known as shifts: periods of feeling more like the target animal, or theriotype."

She looked to her left, and the second panelist said, "We'd like to invite you for a meditation session. Beware, you may not like what you feel. But consider it a test of sorts, so you might know who you truly are."

They hadn't mentioned that other word, *otherkin,* but the third panelist said, "Close your eyes and picture your body filled with energy."

The meditation went on and on as we traveled through doors high in the sky, encountered water and boulders, and walked through forests, among other things. Finally, the time came for the animal to appear.

I suddenly saw a wolf emerging from the trees. The panelist urged us to talk to the animal. "Hello," I said silently to the wolf.

"Hello, Kevin," he said.

"What's your name?" I asked. "Lupus Lykos. Or Loopy for short."

I looked in the reflection of the water in front of me. I saw my human form turning into a wolf's. I felt myself being guided through the forest ahead by the wolf. Suddenly, the trees cleared, and we were in a grassland. Following the cues from the panelist, I felt myself merge with the wolf. I could run at great speeds through the steppes. It was a very long time ago, and there were no humans around.

Then we were guided back down from this higher land into the panel room. I opened my eyes. The panelists talked a bit more about the whole thing, but I felt stunned. It was an epiphany.

Jess and I got on the bus, where we found Luis. We sat across from him. "Fun weekend?" he asked.

"It was interesting," I said. "Hey, Luis, have you ever heard about therianthropy?"

"Oh, yeah."

"Would you consider it a religion?"

He shrugged. "Not really. It's a belief system. Kind of like Buddhism."

I told him about the meditation session. "Sounds like a load of bullshit to me," he said. "My understanding is that if you do identify that way, you're not going to need guided meditation to figure it out."

When we got back to New York, Luis and I added one another on Facebook. He would be heading back to Boston.

That was how I became a werewolf.

9. Two Brazilians

Monday, October 3, 2011

Françoise and I took turns staring at Nate in the middle school cafeteria. He'd been adopted from Brazil as a baby and had beautiful dark skin, hair, and eyes.

Eventually in the 8th grade, Françoise dated him for a little while. They eventually broke up amicably. Once I lamented to her that I had never kissed anyone. "Kiss Nate," she said. "He's a good kisser."

I made it no secret to my friends I was in love with him. Finally, in the 9th grade my friend Amy offered to ask him out for me, which was so unbelievably middle school, but he said yes.

I ran into him after school a couple days later near the front doors. "Kevin!" he shouted tenderly. In my infinite awkwardness, I gave him the sort of hug you would give a friend, not a boyfriend.

We "dated" for 2 months, during which time I barely saw him. At the end of the whole thing, he called me and said, "Kevin, I'm sorry, but I have to break up with you. I know we'll get back together someday, but maybe not for a year or so." I went into my room and collapsed on the bed, laughing. How strange life was.

For many, many years, I couldn't get the thought out of my head, *I could have kissed him.*

I knew another Brazilian in high school. His name was João, but everyone called him Frogger. Unlike Nate, he was born and raised in Brazil, but he attended school in the U.S. for reasons unknown to me. I had a massive crush on him. He was on the same bus, and one day before I got off at my house, I hugged him and kissed him on the cheek.

The next day, our friend Sarah caught me at the beginning of the day and said, "Hey, Kev, I need to talk to you about something later. It's about Frogger." The rest of the day, my heart was practically beating out of my chest. *What was up? Did he return my affection?*

When I saw her again later, she said, "Kev, kissing Frogger? You can't just kiss people. I think you need to apologize to him."

So when I saw him on the bus after school, I said, "Hey, Frogger… I'm sorry about yesterday."

"It's okay," he said. "I just get freaked out."

But I could have kissed Nate.

E. THE STRANGEST OF NOSTALGIA

1. Aesthetic

Sunday, May 1, 2022

I paced the midtown Starbucks. She was sitting at the table with a small notebook. *Say hi,* I implored myself. *Maybe she can be your friend.*

"Hi," I said, sitting down across from her.

"Hi," she said, without looking up at me.

"Are you editing something?"

"I'm writing a story."

"Cool!... I like your aesthetic." She was dressed in steampunk. She looked down at her notebook without a word.

"Sorry to bother you," I said, getting up and leaving.

Later, Helen told me that she probably thought I was hitting on her and felt uncomfortable. It's too bad a man can't talk to a woman without the suspicion of an ulterior motive, but I guess that's the world we live in.

I've often reflected that adulthood should be more like toddlerhood, where you can just walk up to someone and say, "Hey, let's be friends." But then innuendo upon nuances rears its ugly head. Unfortunately, that just means we're all the more isolated.

2. Connections

Sunday, March 1, 2020

I was visiting Annie for the weekend. Red came by. Before he went over to Annie's room, he shook my hand and said gently, "Hey, Kev, my friend… if you're going to smoke, please do it outside. Okay?"

"Sure," I said, slightly embarrassed. "How was the wedding?"

"Oh, it was nice. Saw some people I hadn't seen in a real long time. You know how it goes."

He disappeared into my sister's room. I heard them talking. I decided to smoke a bowl, so I went outside, as Red had suggested. It was an unseasonably warm day. Just then the sun poked through the clouds and I took off my black jacket which was adorned with quite a bit of metal. Underneath I had on a Queen shirt, the famous photograph of the four members that appeared on the cover of their second album, and in the "Bohemian Rhapsody" music video. It was meditative inhaling and exhaling the substance. I had quite a high tolerance by that point, so I was still mostly sober by the time I got back inside.

When I got inside, I heard soft breathing through the door of the sexual kind. I went back outside and waited. A nice breeze blew by.

Eventually, I deemed it safe to reenter. When I did, Red burst through the door in a post-orgasmic glow. "Want to play a round of Icehouse?

"What's that?"

"It's a game our friend Randi taught us once."

Annie came through the door. We sat in a circle, and they taught me the game, which involved colored pyramids, on their sides or standing up, called defenders and attackers.

"To be honest, I'm not very good at this," said Red. We played anyway. Red won the first game, then I won one, then Annie won one. We called it a day after that.

"I have a feeling Matt would like this game," I said.

"Matt?" asked Red.

"Yeah, my best friend, Matt Paciullo."

Red froze. "Paciullo?" he whispered.

"Yeah, that's his last name. Why, do you know him or something?"

"I know his brother, Jim," he said quietly. "I saw him yesterday at the wedding. But it's been many years."

"Oh yeah, Jim. I see him sometimes at their house."

"Their house? Didn't they move years ago?"

"Yeah, their house in Connecticut."

"Oh. I hadn't had any idea where they were living. Say…"

"Yeah?"

"You wouldn't have their address by any chance, would you?"

"I think I do. I'll text it to you, okay?"

"Thank you," he said, still speaking quietly. "I'd appreciate it."

"You're not going to just show up there, are you?"

"No. But there's a little known means of communication known as the post."

Annie yawned. "I'm getting tired," she said.

I was tired too from the pot, so they went into her room, and I settled on the couch.

The next day, I returned to the city.

"Hey, Matt," I said, "my sister's boyfriend is friends with Jim."

"Huh. How about that."

"Yeah, they go way back."

"What's his name?"

"Red. Well, that's not his real name. I forget what his real name is. It's something really complicated."

"I'll mention him to Jim next time I see him."
"No need. I think he's going to write Jim a letter soon."
"Ah. Got it."

3. Solstice Party

Saturday, June 1, 2024

Many years ago, I used to go to a winter solstice party. It was at a house up the road from where Annie and I lived. It was a big affair, the downstairs packed with adults, some of whom had brought musical instruments for a folk jam. Meanwhile, all the kids, meaning high schoolers and college students, hung out upstairs, forming their own little party. Casey, the son of the couple who hosted the party, was always there with his guitar.

Sometimes the guitar would get passed around and everyone got a chance to try it out. There were other amusements: Casey was a whiz with the Rubik's Cube and liked to teach everyone else how to solve it.

After a few years of missing it due to the pandemic, I went back last winter. This time, all the people I used to know, the kids, were downstairs socializing with the adults. I wandered upstairs and into the room where we used to hang out. There were a bunch of little kids—I mean toddlers—playing and amusing themselves.

It was the most profound symbol of the passing of time that I'd ever experienced. The next generation was getting ready to make their way in this world. I felt tremendously sad, but also a tiny bit tender. *Yes, become who we once were.*

4. Correspondence

May 21, 2020

"Dear Jim,

Yes, it's me. It was nice to see you at Amanda and Jack's wedding. I'm sorry I didn't talk to you any more than I did. Honestly, I was surprised to see you there.

How have you been? What have you been up to? I'm afraid my life since college hasn't been too exciting. I've got my baseball (Mets fan), and a comfortable life materially. Sadly, my mother lost a battle with COVID recently, so I'm on my own, except for my girlfriend Annie, whom I've known since I started college.

It's so strange. You were such an important part of my life way back when. And then I suddenly didn't see you for 13 years. What happened when you went away to university? Did something fundamental change?

Please don't ignore this letter. I need to know I still have one small tether to you, however tenuous.

Fondly,

Red"

June 1

Hey, Red!

Frankly, it shocked me a bit too to see you at the wedding, so no worries. I've been good, working at a bank where I live in Maryland.

I'm glad you're doing all right. I saw Annie with you during the vows, and I figured you were an item. You two make a cute couple!

It's true that university changed me a bit. I started going to a lot of parties and doing some drugs, believe it or not. I never meant to abandon you and the others. My life sort of moved on. But when Jack called to invite me to be a groomsman, I had to accept. You may remember that we were childhood best friends.

But since I'm writing you a letter, and now I know about you, I may as well ask about the others. Bones, well, I don't really care about Bones, not since the fiasco with Susan. But how the hell is Ox?

Sincerely,

Jim"

June 4

"Dear Jim,

I was invited to the wedding by Amanda.

I'm so sorry to have to tell you that Ox passed away. He died by suicide several years ago.

But I'm very glad to be back in touch with you. I feel a rough patch in my psyche being healed already.

Warmly,

Red"

5. Helen

Monday, August 23, 2021

I was the second person to arrive in the classroom for the first session of my senior year of college. It was a bit dingy, and they were apparently blasting the A/C because it was very cold. I sat down and glanced at the other student. I went to grade school with him. His name was Ralph.

"Oh, hello," he said.

I waved.

"Do you know who I am?"

"I know exactly who you are," I said. He was wearing black sunglasses, and his short hair was dyed black. "How long have you been going as Tommy Townshend?"

"Since we graduated high school," he said.

I nodded. I felt like I should have more to say to this old classmate of mine, but I didn't. More students shuffled in.

"The Idea of Latin America. Not Latin America, but the *idea*," she said to me as she sat down next to me. "What do you think?"

"Sounds like it could be interesting," I said. "What's your name?" It struck me as interesting that I wanted to know, whereas I couldn't care less about Ralph (*Tommy*, I mean).

"Helen, and you?"

"Kev."

So here was this guy I'd known my entire life, and a girl I'd known for about 1 minute, and it was the latter who fascinated me more. Funny how those things work.

The rest of the students had filtered in and in walked the professor. He was African-American, tall and bald, and dressed smartly. "Hello, class," he said from the front of the room. "My name is Terry."

We began by looking at a map of Latin America, with each country numbered, and were instructed to write in our notebooks the names of every country we recognized. After a few minutes, we went over the answers.

We were then given the syllabus, which was extensive. Key to the readings was Walter Mignolo, an Argentine semiotician.

On the way out, Helen and I caught up with one another and exchanged numbers. We talked about our pasts; I was from Mt. Kisco; she was from Los Angeles. She wanted to experience New York. I told her I would help her out; I'd been living in the city for several years, a senior, and she had just gotten there, a freshman.

I invited her over to my dorm pretty soon thereafter. "There's a lot around here we can't do legally yet. I'm turning 21 in November, and you must be 17 or 18."

"Seventeen," she said. "Turning 18 in October."

"Got it. Fortunately, I dabble in things that aren't legal anyway."

"Like what?"

"I'm talking about pot, Helen. Marijuana. Weed."

"So, you're that into it?"

"Pretty much."

I decided I'd tell her the rest later, about being a wolf, about Rodrigo and Danny, and about my dog, who was living with my mom. Instead, I said, "I'll have to introduce you to Matt, too. He's a good friend of mine here. You 2 would get along."

"Sounds good."

The next time I saw Matt, I said, "Hey, so I met a girl named Helen. We've become fast friends."

"Oh, yeah? What's she like?"

I paused and thought for a moment. "She's young and spunky. Definitely of a different generation. I feel like you and I arrived at the end of an era. She's part of the new movement."

"Everyone says that, Kev. We all arrived at the end of an era. How we long for those bygone days."

"Yes, but what I'm saying is Helen is part of the new mankind or womankind, if you will. I don't lament my status as part of an aftershock when there's all this new energy coming forth from this girl. It's very refreshing. In fact..." I paused. "In fact, you know my sister and her boyfriend? I think it's the same with them. She's a few years younger than him, too."

"This is the boyfriend who knows my brother Jim, right?"

"Yep. He's called Red. His real name is... Z... Zb... I forget. It starts with a 'Z' and then another consonant. I think it's Polish."

"Interesting. Well, anyway, I'd like to meet Helen."

"Yeah! Maybe the three of us can go do something. Like get food at the diner sometime."

"Sounds good to me."

I told Helen of this plan, and she was on board.

6. Movies

Saturday, January 26, 2019

I was standing alone in front of the IFC Center on a freezing winter's evening. I didn't know why I was there, other than to catch a movie. I guess that much must be obvious. But there was no other motive behind it.

Suddenly, I spotted two figures approaching, their black trench coats billowing in the wind. As they came nearer, I saw that it was my classmate Matt, although I didn't know him well, and a somewhat older guy who looked like him, but with a decent sized, waxed mustache.

"Oh, hey," I said.

"Hey, there. Kevin, right?"

"And you're Matt. You can call me Kev, by the way."

"Well, thank you! And this is my oldest brother, Rich."

"Here for a movie, I guess?"

"We're watching *The Big Lebowski*," said Rich. "We always come to see that."

"Care to join us?" asked Matt.

"Of course!"

We sat in the back of the theater. We were the only ones there.

"Ever seen this?" asked Rich.

"Nope."

"Ho ho, boy." He left it at that. The flick came on and the brothers kept yelling out lines at the screen as the characters said them. It would have been annoying if it weren't so funny. I enjoyed it overall. Afterward, we walked out of the theater into the frigid night. There was that rare mood of camaraderie, of a budding closeness between friends.

"I'll see you later," said Matt, and stuck out his leather gloved hand. I shook it.

"Later," said Rich. They left, their trench coats once again billowing.

I went back to that movie theater many times, but no one I knew was ever there. I contemplated watching *The Big Lebowski* again but didn't. I kept hoping Matt and Rich would show up. Instead. I stood in the cold and wind all alone all winter. It was an incredibly, profoundly lonely feeling.

Matt and I ended up being in more of the same classes, as he was also studying anthropology, and we got to know one another better. I saw Rich again sometimes when I visited the Paciullo house in Connecticut, but I only got to meet the middle brother, Jim, once or twice.

7. Diner

Sunday, October 3, 2021

We got on the L train, taking us to Montrose Ave. Champs was right around the corner.

"This is my favorite restaurant of all time," I said to Helen. It was a vegan diner. The menu had all the typical diner food, but it was all vegan.

"Are you vegan?" she asked.

"Mostly," I replied. "I do my best. If I'm somewhere and there's a vegan option on the menu, I'll choose that option. This place is a bonanza."

We sat down. I decided to break the ice. "I made a salad, but it was too dry. That was a situation that needed a dressing."

Matt jumped in. "I was working at this diner where the servers kept coming and going. I was in the kitchen with the manager, and I pointed to a dessert on the shelf. 'You need to move that pastry to a lower shelf,' I said.

'What?'

"'I said, you need to move that pastry to a lower shelf. Your problem is you have high turnover.'"

We stared at Helen, who did not react.

"Anything?" I asked, and she finally exhaled and smiled.

"Thank you," Matt said, exasperated.

I ordered the cauliflower wings with angry sauce and a coffee. Matt ordered a TLT (tempeh, lettuce, and tomato). Helen ordered a cheeseburger—the vegan version, of course.

"I do enjoy a vegan creation from time to time, el oh el," she said. Exactly like that: She pronounced the acronym *lol* out loud, *el oh el.*

Our food came quickly. My wings were delicious, but the

sauce wasn't spicy enough. "They call this angry sauce, but it isn't, really," I said.

"Is it even morning grumbles sauce?" Matt asked.

"Not even that," I said.

I sipped my coffee. "You should know that Kev is a caf-fiend," Matt said to Helen.

"Oh yeah," I said. "One of my many vices." Between bites, I said with my mouth full, "I wonder if you can alkalinize coffee."

"You wonder if you can alcoholize coffee?" asked Helen and laughed.

I swallowed. "Alkalinize."

"I thought he said aerosolize," said Matt. "Yes, let us aerosolize coffee." He pretended to spray coffee into his nose. We all laughed.

I finished my coffee and ordered a refill. The waiter came and obsequiously filled my mug. We were quiet as we finished our food, and I downed my second coffee.

The next day, I called Matt. "Brunch yesterday wasn't too awkward, was it?" I asked.

"I don't think so. I had fun. It was fun, right? An outhangage threesome."

I snorted. "*Outhangage threesome.*"

"Really, I had fun. It's nice hanging out with another person sometimes. Didn't you have fun?"

"I did," I said.

8. Instant Replays from the Exodus

Tuesday, August 6, 2019

Red and Annie sat at a table at Starbucks. Red was sipping an almond milk latte. Annie had in front of her an iced matcha latte.

"I think I came up with a title," Red finished his sip and said.

"For the story?" Annie asked.

"Yes."

"The one you've been working on since you were 19?"

"Yes. Can I run it by you?"

"Of course."

"Okay, and tell me if this is too pretentious: *Instant Replays of the Exodus.*"

She thought. "Where did that come from?"

"Well, it's about the diaspora from Quincy, right? But it's very 21st century."

"Maybe *from,* instead of *of?* Instant Replays *from* the Exodus?"

"Yeah! That sounds a little less pretentious somehow."

9. Graduation, Part 2

Wednesday, May 18, 2022

It was to take place at Radio City Music Hall, the grand event. We were all gathered like cattle in the basement as they organized us alphabetically. I was in the "D" section, for Davies. Matt was in the "P"'s, for Paciullo. Once we were in order and the time came, we marched upstairs to "Pomp and Circumstance" for the Steinhardt School baccalaureate ceremony.

In the audience, among the throng I saw my mom, my sister Annie, and her fiancé Zbigniew, although people usually called him Red. Next to them were Jamie, Jocelyn, Rich, and Jim. Helen couldn't make it for whatever reason, or didn't want to, although she promised to come over to Red's house later.

Afterward, I got into the passenger seat of my mom's car in the parking garage. Annie and Red sat in the back. We had already cleared out all the stuff from my dorm, so this was my good-bye to the city for now.

As we drove up the West Side Highway, I gazed out the window. All those buildings, reaching up for the sky, so impersonal yet welcoming. New York ceded to Yonkers and then things began to get less dense. Eventually we arrived in Mt. Kisco.

"Hey, Z," my mom said as we sat on 2 couches in our living room, eating cheese and drinking wine. "Are you going to see your friend Jim anytime soon? I noticed him and his family there next to us."

"Did you guys introduce yourselves?" asked Red.

"Oh, of course," she said. "We know Kev is close with Matt. We struck up a conversation with them once you pointed them out. What a coincidence we were all sitting together!"

"Anyway, to answer your question, I still haven't spoken to

Jim in person since Amanda's wedding 2 years ago."

"Don't you think you should reach out?" my mom said.

"I'm not sure. It's been so long. I don't even know if he's the same person anymore. I don't even know if *I* am."

10. That Night

Wednesday, May 18, 2022

That night, Red sat in front of his computer and loaded Facebook. He typed in the search bar: Jim Paciullo. The first result sure was him. He started to write a message:

"Dear Jim,

I noticed you sitting next to us at Kev and Matt's graduation. I never heard back from you after my last letter, so I thought I'd reach out. Let me know if you're ever in town. Maybe we could grab coffee or something." He stared at it for about 3 full minutes, then deleted it.

How strange, he reflected as he lay in bed. *You could lose everything, but once you finally had the chance to get it back, you realized that it wasn't there anymore for the taking.*

11. The Paciullo House

Friday, April 15, 2022

The house was on a quiet suburban street in southwestern Connecticut, the kind where nobody bothers to lock their front door. You could take the New Haven Line to Greenwich, then you were close enough for somebody to come pick you up, Rich usually. Or sometimes you could get a ride from Westchester if someone was willing.

This time Matt and I had taken the train from the city. We waited in front of the station in the pleasant April evening weather. We were going to graduate from NYU in a little less than a month.

"So, what are you going to do?" Matt asked. "After we graduate?"

"Probably keep studying," I said. "I want to get my master's, maybe more."

"Well, you always were a better student than I was. How you gonna pay for that all? Take out a loan or something?"

"Well… actually… my mom is funding my schooling."

"Oh, lucky. Say, whatever happened to your dad?"

"He left a long time ago." I didn't elaborate. After a pause, I said, "How about you? What are you going to do?"

"Well, Jim moved to Maryland after college and works for a bank."

"What about Rich?"

"Rich…" He paused. "Rich isn't up to much these days."

A car pulled up, loud with music. "Speak of the devil," said Matt.

Matt got in the passenger's seat, and I got in the back. Rich paused the CD player. "What have you got playing today?" Matt asked.

"I'm getting heavy into Obituary. I can't believe I'd never heard *The End Complete* before." He hit "play," and we were off. It was only about a 15-minute drive to the house. The music was deafening, but I didn't mind.

We pulled into the driveway and got out. The door was unlocked. On the other side was their father. He had long dark hair, like his oldest son. "Rich, Matt," he said. Then he looked at me and said, "Hey, kiddo," and fist bumped me. "Mr. Kevin," called their mother from the kitchen. I walked over, and she gave me a hug. "I see you've come to join us for dinner."

"Ah," I said. "Yes, of course." I'd had no idea.

"Well, I know you're vegan, so I've got something special cooking."

"You know, my mom went to culinary school once upon a time," Matt said.

"Which one?" I asked, and Rich told me. "Huh," I said. "Same one as Matthew."

"Matt went to culinary school now?" asked Jamie, confused.

"No, not Matt. Matthew. Somebody… I once knew." Matt smiled a secretive sort of smile.

"Well, sit down, sit down," Jocelyn said, and we did. She brought out a salad, and we served ourselves. I tried to figure out whether I should put my napkin in my lap or not—silly, I felt, because what if you had to wipe your mouth? Luckily, nobody else was doing it.

I said as we ate, "Did you know that my sister's fiancé went to high school with Jim?"

"Oh, what a coincidence," Jamie said. What's his name?"

"Zbigniew, but everyone calls him Red because he dyes his hair red."

"Sounds vaguely familiar," he said, looking at his wife inquisitively.

"I remember... Skully? Was it?" she said, thinking. "And another one, was it... Ox? I really don't remember, it was so long ago."

"I have no idea," I said. "I just know that he knew Red."

"Jim didn't really keep up with many of his childhood friends, I'm afraid," said Jamie. "He was eager to get out of there."

"As were we," remarked Rich.

Jocelyn got up and went into the kitchen briefly and brought back a large dish. "I made jerk seitan!"

"Jerk Satan?" asked Matt playfully.

"Oh, shush. You've had this before."

It looked delicious, and I couldn't wait to bite into it.

"She makes it herself, you know," said Jamie. "The seitan."

"It's way cheaper than buying it at Trader Joe's," she said.

I mixed a little bit of it with the rice and tasted it. It was as good as it looked.

When we were finished, Rich said, "May we be excused?"

"Of course, honey," said his mom.

As we got up, I said to her, "Thanks for thinking of me. It was delicious." She smiled.

I followed Rich and Matt into Matt's room. They sat on his bed, I sat cross-legged on the floor across from them.

"So, I was thinking," said Rich. "Albums with penises on the cover. *Nevermind. Bagged and Boarded.* Any others?"

"Wasn't there that one that literally had the name of the album drawn in marker on a boner?"

"I think so. But which band was that?"

"I don't remember."

The conversation continued in bizarre fashion, in a manner I imagined only possible between brothers. I didn't really know for sure, only having had a sister.

"What do you think is the most underrated album of all

time?" Rich asked me.

"Hmm. Probably *Amnesiac.*"

"Good choice, good choice. You know, the execs all thought *Kid A* would bomb."

"Yes, because it leaked."

Rich nodded. "Guy knows his stuff," he said to Matt.

"Rich, do you smoke?" I asked suddenly.

"What, you mean cigarettes?"

"No, no. Ganja. You know."

"Oh. No, I don't."

There was an awkward pause. "You can blame me for that question," said Matt finally.

"Well, it's getting late, isn't it?" said Rich, getting up.

"Yes," said Matt and got up, too. He grabbed a sleeping bag and a pillow from his closet.

"Night," said Rich, exiting.

"Good night," said Matt, turning off the light and getting into his bed.

"Good night," I said, settling into my sleeping bag. As I tried to fall asleep, I realized that Matt hadn't given me an answer when I asked what he'd planned to do after college.

12. In Between Years

Thursday, May 19, 2022

"What have you been up to all these years, anyway?" Helen asked Red. "I mean, it's been 8 years since you graduated from the college, right?"

We sat on Red's modest couch, him, Annie, Helen, and me. It was made of old brown leather that was cracked and looked like it was threatening to collapse into itself.

"Um." He sighed. "You're 21, right?"

"Yes," she lied.

"Good." He got up and poured something in the kitchen. Annie got up too and joined him. They brought out a round of liquor on coasters and set the drinks down on the coffee table.

"What's this?" I asked.

"Scotch. And it's good."

I certainly wasn't going to refuse it. Red gulped down half of his right away.

"Helen," he said, "I've had a very boring life. Of course, I experienced the fleeting glory of youth once upon a time. When I was in high school, I had a few good friends. One of them killed himself. One of them I had a falling out with. And one of them disappeared. I knew some folks at the college, too. I roomed with a guy who's now a woman. And of course, Annie." He gulped down the rest of his shot.

"I'm financially comfortable. My mom took care of me until she died of COVID. Yes, I'm a Momma's boy. Or was one, anyway. When she died, I got the house and her IRA. So, you might be asking, what have I done to occupy my time? Well, I'm working on a novel. The working title is *Instant Replays from the Exodus.* It's about someone, based on myself, who finds that all his childhood friends disperse geographically as they come of age and the profound loneliness that results from that.

"And I've been loving Annie. We've been together for 8-and-a-half years, and it was only a matter of time before we got engaged." He sighed again. "I'm turning 31 in the fall, Helen. My 20s were just a nothing decade. Frankly, I don't see things changing much. But you have to count your blessings. I'm safe here. I've got Annie. You'll find as you get older your social circle shrinks like a sponge getting wrung out.

"Everything gets tighter. You see, I had the opportunity to get back in touch with a friend who disappeared. You know him—his name is Jim Paciullo. But Jim and I no longer exist as the human beings who existed 11 years ago. Everything is changed and different now. So, you just have to be happy with what you've got. And I've got this house, and I've got Annie."

Helen sipped her scotch. "That seems like an awful lot of time to be working on a novel. But you do you."

"Hey," said Annie, "how about a few rounds of Icehouse?"

"What's Icehouse?" asked Helen.

"It's a game our friend Randi taught us back in college. Kev knows how to play, too."

We explained the rules to Helen. Four-person Icehouse was a little different from three-person Icehouse, a little more complicated. Defenders and attackers, as usual. Helen won the first round. "Beginner's luck," said Red sourly. We played a few more rounds, then Helen decided she'd had enough.

Red drove us to the train station, where we boarded the Metro North. I got off at Mt. Kisco. Helen would be traveling all the way into the city. I probably wouldn't see her again for a long time, so I gave her a big hug. My mom came and picked me up.

F. BOYFRIENDS

1. Timeline

Thursday, July 15, 2021

"So let me get this straight," said Helen as we strolled through Washington Square Park. It was a hot day and there was birdsong in the air. "You visited Matthew in your second semester at NYU. Then you dated Dragon Man, Rodrigo, I mean, as a sophomore, and then Danny as a junior this past year?"

"That's right," I said. "On either side of the pandemic."

"Okay. Just trying to keep track of it all. And now you have your cat… Kr… K…"

"Krzysztof. That's right. I adopted him the summer before this year, and he's currently living with my mom with the understanding I'll take care of him once I graduate."

"How did you come up with that name, anyway?"

"It started out as a joke. Anytime I visited Starbucks, I got tired of telling them my name was Kevin. So instead I began saying 'Krzysztof.' I always loved it when they asked me how it was spelled. I loved seeing the befuddled expressions on their faces. So, when I got my cat, it just seemed like the right name."

"I'll bet he's cute. A kitten, still?"

"Actually, he was 5 when I got him. He'd been living at the shelter a whole year."

"Wow."

"I guess nobody wanted him. He was obese. But since last summer, he's lost all the weight."

"Does he go outside?"

"Oh, yeah. He wanders all around the neighborhood. He's very good about coming in when it gets dark, though, so we're not concerned."

"Orange tabby, you said?"

"Yep."

She wouldn't meet him until the following summer, after I had graduated.

2. Dragon, Part 1

Saturday, September 14, 2019

"Hey Luis, do you know of any other furries in New York?" I typed from my dorm room.

"Maybe. I'm more apprised of the Boston scene, but I could give you a name or two."

"Oh cool, like who?"

There was a pause. Then I saw that he was typing again. "There's someone I know from way back. He's a dragon, actually, a scalie, as they're known. I can give you his info, but I have to warn you to be careful."

"Careful? Why?"

"He… can be a handful. I won't say anything more."

"What's his name?"

"Rodrigo."

I got his Skype info, and we began chatting. Rodrigo attended LaGuardia Community College, where he was studying computer science. He lived at home.

I told him about my fursona, Loopy, but he called me "Kevin." His was named Lung, but he preferred that I call him "Rodrigo."

We hit it off, and he suggested we get together that Friday evening. I ended up taking a lengthy combination of subways and buses to East Elmhurst. I saw the sign: *Mama's Empanadas*. I entered and noticed a guy sitting in the corner with his phone. I pulled out my own phone and wrote, "Are you the guy with the glasses?" He looked up and waved. I sat across from him.

"Well, hey there," he said.

"Hi," I said. "I'm Kevin."

"I know," he said and smiled. "I guess I ought to ask, since I don't think I have already, how long have you been in the fandom?"

"You mean the furry fandom? Uh, well, my friend Jess took me to AnthroCon this past year."

"Ah, so you're a newbie."

"I guess so. How about you?"

"Oh, about 10 years." He saw the impressed expression on my face. "Yeah, I'm a real gray-muzzle." He laughed. "I started getting into it as a teenager." I guessed that put him in his mid-20s somewhere. Like my friend Matt had once said, I always seemed to be getting involved with older men. "So, you're studying anthropology?"

"That's correct. Actually, that's what got me into the whole thing. Jess suggested I should study goths and furries. She said that they're not so different: goths like to pretend to be vampires, furries like to pretend to be animals."

"I like that. I go to LGCC. I'm studying computer science."

"I remember."

"Hey, can I buy you a coffee?" he asked.

"Sure." He got up and went to the counter, then came back shortly with two cups of coffee. We sipped quietly.

"Where are you staying tonight?" he suddenly asked quietly and intensely.

"Uh, I guess back at my place. Why?"

"You want to bother with all those buses and subways again?"

"What are you saying?"

He shrugged. "Just that I've got a bedroom that's lonely for one. That's all." I didn't say anything. We finished our coffees. He got up, and so did I. We exited the place.

"Well?" he said. "Want to come with me?"

I hesitated, then said, "Sure." We walked about 4 or 5 blocks and came to a brick rowhouse. He unlocked the door, and we entered. Ahead was a staircase; immediately to the right was another door. He tried to open it, but it was locked. "Fuck," he muttered. He pulled out a credit card from his wallet and jimmied the lock, jiggling the knob until it opened.

"That's pretty badass you can do that," I said.

"It happens. The door locks on its own, and I forgot my key." He descended, and I followed him. At the bottom of the stairs was a large room. There was a fridge, a bathroom, an expansive bed, and a desk with a computer on it.

Suddenly, he gave me a huge hug. He wouldn't let go, but I didn't care. It felt nice. We collapsed together onto his bed. He suddenly laughed and at last surrendered his grasp. His glasses had fallen off, and he grabbed them as he got up.

"I need to work on a program for class," he said, sitting down at his computer. "Make yourself at home." He put on headphones. He seemed absorbed and I was feeling tired—coffee paradoxically does that to me—so I got under the covers and lay there for a little while before I drifted off.

I woke up and he was lying next to me, shirtless. I thought he might awaken eventually, but he was fast asleep. I climbed out of bed, still fully dressed. I grabbed my green messenger bag, but before I left, I noticed two bottles on the desk. I inspected them and one said Suboxone, with a capital *S*. The other said alprazolam, with a lowercase *a*. When I got back to my dorm, I looked them up on my phone. Suboxone was used to treat narcotics addiction. Alprazolam was generic for Xanax, the antianxiety drug. The article I read said that they should never be taken together.

3. Danny, Part 1

Friday, May 7, 2021

Jess had long since transferred from NYU to somewhere out west. Matt wasn't in town, and I was all alone, so I strolled to the Nuyorican Poets' Café. You could always count on that place to provide some entertainment, whether it be slam poetry—which I secretly despised—or jazz. When I got there, a guy was setting up with his acoustic-electric guitar. I sat to listen. He played an open mic set of several songs. He was good at his instrument and had a lovely voice. I noticed that he'd made eye contact several times during the set, so once he packed up and was offstage, I approached him.

"Nice songs," I said.

"Hey, thanks."

"The name's Kevin. Kev, for short."

I'm Daniel. Danny, for short." He smiled. "Want to go somewhere else? Unless you're overly invested in the goings-on of this little café."

We left the place and strolled down the street. "There's something I ought to tell you," he said.

"Yeah? What's that?"

"When I saw you walk into that building, my heart did a somersault."

"Oh," I said.

"I'm sorry," he stammered. "I probably shouldn't have said that."

"No, it's not you," I said. "I've just had some bad experiences in the past."

"Well, if you ever want to talk to me again, here's my card." He handed me his business card and walked away. It said 'Daniel Petrovich, musician and writer,' and had his phone number on it.

4. Dragon, Part 2

I Skyped Rodrigo later that evening. "Hey," I typed.

"Thanks for coming over last night. That made me very happy."

"It was nice."

"Can I ask you something?"

"Sure."

"Can I call you Wolfy?"

"Sure."

A smiley face. "My Wolfy. And you can call me Draggy."

I suddenly felt a jolt of adrenaline that led to my heart. This was really happening.

"Draggy, there's something I want to tell you. I'm not just a run-of-the-mill furry. I'm also a therian."

"Oh? Well, that's good, because I'm otherkin." There was that word! They had mentioned it at AnthroCon, but had never explained it.

"Tell me more."

"I don't know how to explain it, other than to say that sometimes… I can feel my wings. You don't think that's weird, do you?"

"No weirder than being a wolf."

"Can we see each other again next weekend?"

"That would be nice."

The next Friday came around, and I took the same series of subways and buses to East Elmhurst. I texted him I was at his house, and a couple minutes later, he opened the door. I followed him down the staircase to the basement.

"I hope you can stay longer than 1 night this time," he said.

"Sure. I brought all my things, including my laptop."

He smiled and opened his arms. I hugged him. He looked at me, and then he kissed me. It was the first time I had ever kissed someone whom I wanted to kiss.

"Can I ask you something?" I asked.

"What's up?"

"Why are you taking Suboxone?"

He sighed. "I have a troubled past. I'd rather not discuss it."

"And you're taking Xanax, too? Surely the same doctor didn't prescribe both of those."

"I *said*," he said sharply, "I don't want to talk about it."

I was silent. I wanted to change the subject, so I said, "Do you like baseball?"

"Baseball? Don't really know much about it."

"But we're like 5 minutes from Citi Field. You've never watched the Mets play?"

"Nope."

"Maybe I could take you."

He smiled again. "I'd love that."

"They'll be in town next weekend."

Suddenly, there was a loud banging sound on the ceiling and a woman shouting in Spanish. "Dinner time," he said and ran upstairs. He came back down with a plate of chicken and peas. "Sorry, my mom doesn't know about you yet, so we'll have to share this."

"I don't really eat chicken," I said. "Sorry."

"Oh. Well, in that case, do you like Chinese food?"

"Yeah, I do."

"Okay. I have a little money. Come on."

We walked upstairs and outside. Great Wall was a block away. I ordered General Tso's tofu and fried plantains. I don't know why Chinese restaurants always had plantains, but they did. I wanted to pay but Rodrigo insisted. We brought the food back down to his basement, and we each ate our respective dinners.

"Kevin?"

"Rodrigo?"

"Will you be my mate?"

"Mate?"

"You know. Furry speak. My boyfriend."

My face flushed with blood. "Yes," I said, grinning.

He hugged and kissed me.

5. Danny, Part 2

Sunday, May 9, 2021

I dialed the number on the business card. It rang six times. I was certain no one would pick up, but then a voice intoned, "This is Daniel."

"Hey, Danny, it's Kev. Remember? From the café the other night?"

"Ah, yes, of course. You know, I didn't think you'd call. Most people don't."

"So there's more than one of me?"

"I can't say yes or no to that. We've only just met. But I'd like to get to know you better, if that sounds agreeable to you."

"Sure," I said.

"I detect a note of caution in your voice."

"It's just that I had a relationship a couple years ago that ended really badly."

"I'm terribly sorry to hear that. I've had my fair share of those, too."

"Well, would you like to meet up at the Washington Square Starbucks?"

"If you'd indulge me in that, I'd be most flattered."

That evening, I saw him at the Starbucks. I ordered an almond milk latte. When the girl asked my name, I said, "Krzysztof." She stared at her screen for a few moments, then typed something in. She gave me the price, and Danny insisted on paying. He ordered a double espresso.

"So, what's your story?" he asked when we sat.

"I'm from Mt. Kisco in Westchester. I go to NYU now, and I study anthropology."

"How do you like the city?"

"I like it. It's huge and comforting. I need a city to keep me company. Where are you from?"

"Brooklyn. I mean, I was adopted from Russia, but I've always lived in Brooklyn. Do you go out a lot at night?"

"I'm afraid not. I'm neither an early bird nor a night owl. I'm a permanently exhausted pigeon."

He smiled. "Little Pidge."

This was all too familiar to me—I knew what was going to happen. I'd start dating Danny, and I'd end up hurting him. But I somehow felt resigned to fate, so I didn't try to run away from it.

We got up and went outside. He looked at me tenderly. "Can I kiss you?"

Without a word, I complied.

6. A Question of Love

Thursday, July 15, 2021

"The thing is, though, I really did love Rodrigo," I said, continuing our conversation.

"But you didn't love Danny," said Helen.

"No, I never did. I wanted to. But I was terrified I didn't, and I didn't."

"I see."

"Every time I said, 'I love you,' it was a lie. That makes me tremendously sad. But it's also what made me realize that having a boyfriend isn't nearly as important to me as I thought it was."

"Well, at least you know that now."

"Yeah. I went along with everything, all the flirting and the plans, because I thought I needed to be in a relationship, and now that I had one, I didn't want to jeopardize it. I promise you, Helen, I won't do that again."

"Then I'm glad you know that about yourself."

7. Dragon, Part 3

Friday, September 20, 2019

On Wednesday, he Skyped me to say, "Only 2 more days until I get to see you again!"

I arrived Friday evening, and we walked to the bus stop to get to Citi Field, a very short bus ride. As we were walking across the Grand Concourse, there was a car coming, but I had plenty of time to cross the road ahead of it. Rodrigo apparently didn't think so, and he did pretty much the most unhelpful thing possible: He leaned his foot out and tripped me. I crumpled to the ground in a heap. Meanwhile, he put up his hand to get the car to stop. He helped me up, and as we walked the remainder of the crosswalk he scolded, "Do *not* run into traffic like that."

We got to the stadium and there were lots of fans: The team was having a good year. We got tickets for the cheap seats. They were in the left field bleachers, near the foul pole, and they cost $25 each. You could see almost all of the action from there, except when someone hit it down the left field line; then you had to listen to the crowd's reaction to figure out what was happening.

We got to our seats and soon the game began. They were playing Washington. Rodrigo didn't really know the rules, so I was constantly explaining to him what was going on, which I didn't mind in the slightest. For instance, at one point he said, "So… what's a grand slam?"

"It's a home run with the bases loaded," I explained.

At one point, the beer guy came around. I ordered a beer, showing him my fake ID I conveniently had on me. It was a Coors.

Rodrigo got up to go to the bathroom. I wondered if he had brought the Suboxone and/or the Xanax, so I rooted through the bag he'd brought. Yes, both. I suddenly felt the Xanax tempting me. Surely, he wouldn't notice if I snatched just one. I opened the bottle and retrieved one pill. I downed it with the beer. I immediately felt a sense of relaxation come over me. He came back down the stairs. After that, he was much quieter, only occasionally commenting on the progress of the game.

The Mets won, to the delight of the crowd. We filed down to ground level and took the bus back to Rodrigo's house.

When we got there, he said, "I saw what you did."

"What I did?"

"Don't play dumb. Are you fucking insane? Do you know how Whitney Houston died?" He grabbed a sheet of paper with writing on it. "Do you know what this is?"

"What is it?"

"It's a love letter I wrote to you. I was going to give it to you tonight." He grabbed a lighter. "Should I burn it?"

"No, no! I want to read it."

He sighed and dropped the lighter back onto the table. "Fine." He handed it to me. This is what it said:

"Dear Wolfy,

I feel so blessed to have met you at last. I've been waiting for you for 1,000 years, it seems. I already care about you a great deal. The future is looking much brighter now. I hope we have a lot more time together.

Rawr.

Love,

Draggy"

I looked at him and opened my arms. He obliged the hug. Then I said, "I love you."

A tear fell from his right eye. "I love you, too."

8. Danny, Part 3

Friday, May 14, 2021

Danny and I were sitting at the Nuyorican Poets' Café. He handed me a CD in a slim jewel case. He had written on it in red marker, "Pigeon Playlist, Vol. 1."

"What's on it?" I asked.

"Various recordings I've done."

"Oh, cool. Did you go to a studio or something?"

"I have a contract with a label."

"That's impressive."

He shrugged. Before the evening was over, we made out again. I was falling into the rabbit hole.

I listened to the CD when I got home. It was all right, folky tunes with a guitar. I had to admit he had a nice voice.

He asked me out the next day on Skype. I said yes. He said, "Now that we're boyfriends, can I tell you I love you? I'm sure that's what this feeling is." He was infatuated.

"You can say that," I said. "Please don't be offended if I don't return it right away." Eventually, I did return it. I wasn't sure I knew what I was doing.

"Listen," he said one day. "I'm going on a tour this summer, mostly venues in the Tennessee area. I'd love for you to come with me."

"That sounds lovely," I replied, because it was what I knew he wanted to hear. This was all wrong.

"If you think you can handle it," he said cautiously.

"Why wouldn't I be able to handle it?"

He smiled. "Pidge."

9. Dragon, Part 4

Saturday, October 5, 2019

I stayed over at Rodrigo's. We did the usual routine: I arrived, set down my backpack, then he gave me an enormous hug. We held each other for a long time, then things progressed, and we were intimate. Then he went to his computer to work on his programming, and I went to bed.

When I woke, he was next to me. I kept waiting for him to wake up, but he was fast asleep. It was already lunchtime, and I had some money, so I got dressed and left for the Subway on the corner, figuring he would let me back in once he was awake.

As I was eating my sandwich, I got a text from him. It said, "Where the fuck are you?"

"I went to Subway for lunch," I typed back.

"Hold on. I'm coming." I waited for him, and he burst into the Subway. "I'd like to talk to you outside," he said quietly. I looked at my lunch. "Leave the sandwich." We walked out the door. "So, you would really leave me like that," he said sadly.

"What?"

"You would leave me there alone, like everyone always does."

"I went to *lunch!*"

"Does our relationship mean that little to you?"

"You're crazy. You're overreacting. Please calm down."

He sighed. "Let's go back to my house then." I followed him, without the remainder of my sandwich. We got to his house. "Promise me you won't ever leave," he said.

"Okay. I promise."

He went to his computer. I sat on the bed with my laptop and wrote an email to Matt about the afternoon's events. I got a reply quickly. He wrote, "I had little inkling that Rodrigo would be so unstable and possessive. It seems to me as if he had a difficult past." I thought of the Suboxone. "He sounds like trouble," Matt continued. "It may be best to cut your losses."

But I loved him, I thought.

10. Danny, Part 4

Friday, May 21, 2021

I opened a new email.

"Dear Danny,

I really do love you, but I think it might be for the best if we don't see each other anymore. I didn't ever want to kiss you, and I certainly don't want to go to Tennessee with you. In fact, I hardly know you.

You asked me if I thought I could handle being in a relationship with you. Maybe I can't handle it. Maybe I'll never be able to handle it. Maybe I'm happy with my books, my cat, and my baseball.

I wish you all the best, and know that none of this is your fault.

Sincerely,

Kevin"

I stared at it for an eternity, then clicked "send." An hour later, I received a response:

"Kevin:

Everything in your message made sense except the opening. None of what you describe shows me love. That you were even going to bail on Tennessee proves you don't love me.

I don't normally wish restrictions on people, but you absolutely do deserve to be confined to the cloisters of your own mind. And in the future, think very hard before you ever tell someone you love them. I don't believe you meant it.

Daniel"

And that was that.

11. Dragon, Part 5

Sunday, October 6, 2019

The more I sat on that bed, reflecting on things, the more uneasy I felt. He had obviously been using before I met him. He tripped me as I was crossing the street. He threatened to burn his love letter. He flipped out because I went to lunch. It was a battle of heart versus mind. Maybe I could at least take a break from things. I gathered my things into my backpack and got up. He noticed me out of the corner of his eye and got up too. I froze. He moved between me and the staircase.

"What are you doing?"

"I need to think. Elsewhere."

"Please, hon." I tried stepping to his side, but he met my movement. "Please."

I stopped.

"I love you," he said.

I was silent.

"You don't want to say it!" he shouted. He grabbed me by the hand and took me back inside. "I'm begging you. Stay."

I sighed. "Okay. I'll stay here."

"Good," he said and exhaled. He sat at his computer. I sat on the bed, watching him. At one point, he put his headphones on. Good. This was my chance. I grabbed my backpack and managed to very quietly tiptoe out and up the stairs and then out of the building. I hurried to the bus stop and luckily caught the bus just in time. I didn't feel safe until I was on the subway back into Manhattan. I blocked him on Skype. I never wanted to hear from him again.

Later, I realized that I had left my spiky bracelet at Rodrigo's house.

12. Thesis

Friday, May 20, 2022

I wrote my thesis on goths and furries.

PART THREE: JONATHAN

G. WANDERING OFF

1. Ego

Sunday, June 19, 2016

I haven't seen Jim Paciullo in 7 years. After we graduated high school, me, Jim, Ox, and Red (although Red technically got his "Good Enough Diploma"), Jim went off to college and never talked to us again. It didn't surprise me Jim didn't want to see me, after what happened at Susan's house, but I thought he'd keep up with the others.

I guess that's what happens. You could be friends with someone, dear friends, but those 2 people over time cease to exist, making any reunion totally and absolutely impossible.

I really feel there's very little of my ego left. It's been battered by the winds of depression, anxiety, and panic, to the point where I'm a tree without its leaves, a dying dandelion with its fuzz blown to the heavens by some little boy or girl.

2. Ox, Part 1

Sunday, September 21, 2014

I was at my sister Kayla's house. She flipped through the newspaper. Suddenly, she stopped.

"Hey, Jon, didn't you know a Connor Byrne?"

"Yes. Why?"

She handed me the paper. It was turned to the obituaries. She pointed.

"Connor Byrne, of Quincy, New York, passed away on Wednesday at the age of 23. He leaves behind his mother, Colleen Stone-Byrne. There will be no public memorial."

"Oh, God," I said quietly.

When I had a private moment, I pulled out my phone and called the Byrne house. I amazingly still had their number.

"Hello?" came a female voice.

"Hi, Colleen? This is Jonathan Bonifacio. You know me as Bones."

"Oh, hello, dear. How are you?"

"I'm okay. But listen, I just heard about your son and I'm so, so sorry."

"Thank you, Bones. That means a lot to me."

"Colleen…"

"Yes?"

"It was suicide, wasn't it?"

"It was. He hanged himself with a shower line."

I sighed. "Okay. I wish you all the best in this difficult time."

"Thank you, honey."

I hung up. So old Ox had done himself in. In a sense, it wasn't that surprising. After all, his very nickname came from "Awks," the Awkward One. He never seemed to fit in. I reflected that there were a lot of similarities between him and me. The big difference was that I could never kill myself. I'm far too stubborn.

However, I must say that I'm glad I didn't own a gun. That would make things far too easy. If you're going to hang yourself, like Ox had, you had to deliberate over it. You had to really want to do it. With a gun, assuming it's loaded, and the safety is off, all you need is one twitch of a finger. One minute gesture, and there comes the round out of its chamber and into your skull, and that's that. If I had a gun, I seriously doubt I'd still be around.

3. Rock Club

Friday, June 4, 2004

When I was in the 7th grade, two years before I met Jim, I was leaving science class one day when I overheard a conversation between Will Vinogradov and Louis Chambers. Will told him how he had been writing songs, but he didn't have anyone to practice with. Louis told him he couldn't help, as he didn't have a musical bone in his body.

I approached Will in the hallway. "Hey, I heard you need someone to jam with. I play the drums, you know."

"Oh! That's cool! You should come over sometime. I've got a drum set. Where do you live?"

I told him, and he didn't live far away, within biking distance. So that weekend I biked over.

He lived in an old house with a brother, a sister, and two parents. There were two upright pianos in their living room and all other sorts of musical instruments strewn about and in cases, including guitars.

"We're a musical family," Will said. "I've just started writing songs. Do you want to hear?"

"Sure."

He sat down at a piano and played. He sang, "I went to ShopRite, I saw a lady, she was angry, 'cause the deli was closed. The second I saw her, she called me a porker… 'cause the deli was closed." His playing intensified, and he said, "Second verse," then sang, "She called me a porkie, a dirty little porkie, a salted little porkie… you don't even know me! So come and show me! Why I'm a porkie! 'Cause the deli was closed!" He finished playing. "Now let's try it with you on the drums."

I obeyed, and we got through the song to our mutual satisfaction.

"So, what should we call that?" I asked. 'The Porker Song'?"

"Nah. How about for now… 'Song A.'"

"You know, as I was biking over, there was a sign saying that a section of road was sponsored by the Quincy Democrats. Maybe we should sponsor a section of road. Then we could get them to put up a sign saying, 'The next 1.5 miles are sponsored by The International Federation of Porkers.'"

"What does that make us?" Will asked. "The International Federation of Porkers Players?"

"Yes, that. I love it."

We became fast friends. I visited his house often after that. I'd bike over and spend the night. We watched movies together. We were fond of *Napoleon Dynamite*, *School of Rock*, *Dodgeball*, and even the original *Oliver!*, among others.

The next year, Will joined the middle school rock club. I didn't. He played the guitar. They had their concert, and it was okay. I had numerous friends involved. The next Monday, at the beginning of school, before homeroom, a girl I sort of knew named Lisa approached me and said, "Are you… close? With Will?"

"Yeah, we're good friends."

"Want to come to the rock club party on Friday? It's at my house."

"Sure!"

So on Friday, I got my dad to drive me to Lisa's house. It was a very tame party, just a bunch of 8th graders supervised by a couple of middle school music teachers. I soon got bored. I felt like getting some exercise, so I left the house and strolled to the top of the hill. I walked around the neighborhood for a while, just wandering. Eventually, I circled back down to the hill. A man stood there. "I think some people are looking for you," he said. When I got to the bottom, everyone came running toward me, shouting my name.

"There you are!" said Miss Deacon shortly. "Where in the world were you?"

"I… took a walk."

"Well, because of you, we've spent the last 40 minutes searching for you instead of celebrating our accomplishments as the rock club, *which you aren't even a part of.*"

"I think you need to call your parents to come get you," said Mr. Petrosian. I called them from the house phone. My dad arrived to pick me up.

On Monday, Will told me, "You know, Lisa and I told them to let you stay at the party. I'm sorry they kicked you out."

"Thanks."

When we got to high school, Will and I drifted apart. He was into the music scene, whereas I'd become friends with Jim and Ox and Red, the weirdos. When we graduated, in the yearbook Will was awarded most musical and also smartest. We all campaigned for Red to be named smartest, as he really deserved it, but the administrators wouldn't allow it, because he technically didn't graduate.

4. Bike Trail

Sunday, August 4, 2002

My mom, my dad, and I were on our way to the bike trail. Kayla wasn't with us: She was a teenaged girl and was concerned about being seen with her parents in public.

We arrived and got out of the car. It was hot and very muggy, even in the late afternoon when the sun wasn't at its strongest.

My mom said out of nowhere, "Jon, I happened to look at your browser history yesterday. And… I know you're at an age when you're curious, but… why are you looking at porn sites?"

I was 11, and I felt the hot blood rush to my face as I blushed. Hadn't she just said it? I was at an age when I was curious. I didn't care about sex—I just knew I really liked looking at vaginas.

I said nothing. My dad said, "Lucille, I'll talk to him later about this, okay?" She nodded her head solemnly.

My dad and I took our bikes down from the car. My mom wanted to walk. He and I rode our bikes some way to the first bench. We often used to ride around town, but the trail was totally flat, ideal for cycling.

When we got there, he said, "Hey, Jonathan. For your mother's sake, your sake, and my sake, delete your history when you're done on the computer. Okay?" He smiled. I smiled back.

I told him I wasn't ready to turn back: I wanted to go a little farther. He agreed and said he would be waiting by the bench. I biked to the next bench and back. When I got back, my dad wasn't there. I was totally bewildered. Where had he gone? I waited. I waited some more. Then I panicked. "Dad?" I shouted into the trees. "Dad?"

Maybe he had gone in the same direction, I thought. I got on my bike and pedaled all the way to the next road crossing. There were some teenagers there, milling about. One of them said, "Hey, kid, where's your helmet?" I realized I had forgotten it.

I turned around. By this point, my legs were very tired, and I had to walk. It was getting dark now, and I was totally scared. As I got to the other bench where I had left my helmet, I saw two bright lights approaching. Oh, God, was it the police?

It turned out to be my parents. My dad had somehow maneuvered the car around the posts that served to keep motor vehicles off the trail. Everyone was upset, but we didn't say anything. We got home to a dark house. "I did *not* expect to be getting back this late," my mom said crossly.

5. Susan's House, Part 1

Tuesday, June 16, 2009

My sister Kayla had grown up with a guy named Sven. Jim's older brother Rich knew them, too. They all used to hang out at Sven's mom Susan's house, and Jim was often there too, so I frequently found myself there. It was a little house in the woods. In front was a circle with comfortable chairs and swinging benches. There were various bird feeders and the summer birds all visited, cardinals, blue jays and the like. She even had a red hummingbird feeder that saw traffic.

I strongly felt they would all get along with Red. As for Ox, he wasn't very social. But Red was an outgoing guy, and I was closer with him, anyway. I invited him over for Susan's 50th birthday. Sven was very glad to meet him, and immediately questioned him about auditioning for the Renaissance Faire. He said he'd consider it. I stayed the night there, as I so often had.

It came time for auditions. Rich would take Red in his own car while Susan drove Sven, Kayla, and me. Then tragedy struck. My dad asked Kayla to come over to our house. There was something he needed to tell us. "You know Grammy had a stroke last week," he said. "And that she tried to walk again." He sighed. "I received word today that she had another stroke. A much worse one. And… she's not going to walk. She's not going to live." The three of us joined in a tight group hug and cried together.

She died soon after, and we flew to Florida for a private family memorial. I saw a great number of family members whom I had not seen in a very long time. I guess that's how it works. If you want to see someone close to you, wait until a wedding or funeral.

When I got back, the next time I was at Susan's house, Sven motioned to speak to me out of earshot from the others. "I have something troubling to report," he said. "Susan, Rich, and I heard Red say he was glad your grandmother had died, so he could get a ride to the Faire the other day."

I was alone with Jim later and told him what Sven had said. "I don't think I feel comfortable having him over here again," I said.

"I wouldn't burn that bridge if I were you. Red is a good guy. I'm sure he didn't mean anything bad by that."

"Didn't mean anything bad? He said he was *glad* my grand-mother died, Jim."

"I still think it's a misunderstanding." We left it at that.

It was summertime. Graduation had passed: it was truly the end of an era. I ran into Red at the café in town one day. He was happy to see me. "I have to tell you, Bones, I've decided I'm not going to do the Renaissance Faire. I want to focus on school. As you know, I'm going to community college."

"You're going to take the GED exam?"

"Already did, my friend. It was a fucking joke."

"Listen, Red. I'd prefer you not come back to Susan's."

"Oh? Why's that?"

I chose my words carefully. "I don't think the scene's for you."

He was visibly disappointed. "I'm sorry to hear you say that."

The next time I was at Susan's house, Jim was there. "Hey," he said. "You should invite Red over here again sometime. Or even Ox. It would be like a last meeting before we go our separate ways."

"You know how I feel about Red," I said. "I told him not to come here anymore."

"I told you not to kick Red out of this house!" Jim yelled at me, suddenly angry. I had never heard him take that tone before. "Listen," he said. "The three of us are going off to college in a couple months. I thought we could hang out one last time, but I guess not."

"I'm sorry," was all I could say.

As it turns out, I haven't seen Jim again since that day.

6. Fire Drill

Friday, August 28, 2009

After high school, I found myself at Melville College, in western Massachusetts. It was a small school, buildings nestled in between an idyllic splash of trees and lakes. In my first days there, I tried my best to make friends. To that end, I found myself in the woods smoking pot with some other guys. I got back to my dorm, and my roommate Harry said, excited, "Are you high?" I nodded. Actually, I had no idea if I was high or not. I had never done it before, and I wasn't sure how I was supposed to feel.

I woke up that night to the light on and 2 men standing over me. I realized that the fire alarm blared. They'd tried to rouse me, but I kept falling back asleep. I've always been an exceptionally sound sleeper.

The next day, Kyle Johnson, director of resident services, showed up in my room with one of the other men from the previous night. "I was informed by some other students you've been smoking marijuana," he announced.

I made my best confused face, which probably looked totally fake. "Well, I haven't."

"We need to search your room." Search it they did. I had nothing on me, so once they had turned over everything, they left.

Apparently, they called my dad, because I got an email later that day he had blind copied me on. It said:

"Dear Mr. Johnson:

You have accused my son of violating a federal statute. My son has not done as much as touch a drop of liquor in his young life, let alone smoke marijuana. I'm not spending the amount of money I am for him to be harassed. I expect you and your staff to leave him alone moving forward.

Sincerely,

Robert Bonifacio"

They decided in case there was a real fire, I'd need to be on a ground floor dorm rather than the second floor, so I could be safely evacuated. The only available room was in another building, with a Russian exchange student, Alexei. He didn't speak much English yet, and this was the beginning of a terribly lonely time for me. While everyone else was off socializing and hanging out, I was in my room or the library, reading. I had a nameplate outside my room with my name on it. One day in December I heard two guys walking by. The following was their exchange:

"Jonathan Bonifacio. Who the fuck is Jonathan Bonifacio?"

"I don't know! No one knows." That was the worst moment of my life.

7. Math

Wednesday, June 8, 2005

The bus stopped at the park in New Jersey. I was the only kid who didn't have a lunch packed: My mom had forgotten. I was forced to poke around like a beggar for people who would give me scraps of their food.

We got to our hotel in the suburbs of D.C. I had been packed in a room with 3 kids I didn't know. The class had actually been divided into 2 trips. My best friend back in 8th grade, Will, was on the other trip.

One day, we visited the Holocaust Museum. There had been a problem obtaining the tickets, so we had less time than we were supposed to have had.

Being of Sephardic Jewish heritage myself, I was very interested in the various exhibits. I made my way to the top floor and made sure to carefully read all the text and look at all the photographs.

The next thing I knew, I noticed 2 men approach me. One was the teacher in charge of the trip. I didn't recognize the other. The latter commented quietly, "Hey, he was actually reading the exhibits." Mr. Ferguson was furious. He told me to follow him.

We walked across the city toward the American Museum, which was the next stop. "Why in the world didn't you get on the bus with everyone else?" he shouted.

"I didn't know what time it was," I said.

"You didn't have a watch?"

"No."

"Then why weren't you with someone who did?" The answer was I didn't actually have any friends whom I could have buddied up with. I didn't say anything.

I sat in the cafeteria with Mr. Ferguson, another teacher, and the school cop, who was with the trip. "Do you happen to know Rebecca Painter?" the other teacher asked.

I was surprised. "Yes, actually I do."

We were in some of the same classes. "Were you two goofing off together?" I was totally confused. "You know that she missed the bus, too?" I had no idea. Apparently, she had come running out of the building as the bus had started to pull away, and they stopped in time, whereas I had somehow missed the bus by a good 40 minutes.

"What do you think the odds are?" said Mr. Ferguson. "Officer, what do you think the odds are that 2 people who know each other would just happen to both miss the bus?"

The cop looked at me and said, "I dunno." He shrugged and pointed at me. "Isn't he the one who's supposed to be good in math?"

Classic, I thought. I couldn't wait to share that with my dad.

For many years after that, anytime we were in any situation that required basic math, even counting something up, my dad would say, "Aren't you the one who's supposed to be good in math?"

8. Andrea

Friday, December 25, 2009

"And they had no idea who I even was." I was home for Christmas, and I was relating to my dad what had happened the previous week.

He thought for a while with a pensive look on his face. "They didn't know who Jonathan Bonifacio was?"

"That's right."

"Didn't your friends in high school call you Bones?"

"Yeah."

"Maybe you ought to go as that instead from now on. If you've got a persona that works, stick with it."

I took his advice and posted a Jolly Roger outside my door when I got back in January, and the word "Bones" in bold type. I wore my skull and bones beanie again I'd found in the closet of my childhood bedroom.

Andrea was getting her BFA in painting. She used to paint outside on the lawn by my dorm, which is how we met that spring. I wandered over to her easel and sat down. She was working on a landscape of the view that looked out over the hill, the trees and lakes.

"I haven't seen you around here much," she said.

"I keep myself scarce."

"Are you new? What are you studying?"

"I'm a puny freshman, undecided in major."

"That hat… oh! You're the kid who lives with the Russian guy."

"That's right!" Finally, I had someone to eat lunch with.

Unfortunately, I had gradually stopped going to classes. My tenure at Melville College seemed tenuous. I don't think I was mature enough for a post-secondary education curriculum. Since

I didn't go to classes, I never met anyone who made it worth it to stay, until Andrea, and by then, it was too late.

One night, Alexei, whose English had improved greatly, pulled a bottle out from under his bed. "Whiskey," he said. I had no idea why it was blue. I followed him out to the back of a field on the far side of campus, where we met up with a few other guys. We passed the bottle around.

At one point my roommate intoned, "Tomorrow! I have driving practice! Four hours! My instructor say, 'You drink?' I say, 'Don't worry: I'm Russian!'"

We all cracked up.

At one point one of the guys wanted to go home. Alexei insisted he stay. "You leave, I call the college, you drunk." He pulled out his phone. "Yes, college? I'm with Timothy. He drunk." Nobody knew if he was serious, or if he was putting us on. He put his phone back in his pocket: He had been fooling with us. Timothy stayed.

When we finally got back to the dorm room, I lay on my bed and the room spun in circles, I was so fucking drunk. Fortunately, I was at that magical age when you can get fucking drunk as hell and feel no ill effects—no throwing up, no headache the next morning.

I sat with Andrea in the cafeteria one day. "So, you must be pretty serious about painting, then," I said.

"Of course. After this, I intend to go back to Illinois to work on my art."

"You're from Illinois?"

"Plano."

"How are you going to support yourself?"

"I know someone I can stay with. Bones, promise me you'll visit."

"I'll do my best. Either way, we should stay in touch."

I was quite literally failing out of the college. I spent my free time reading. The only final exams I even bothered to show up for were German and music theory. My parents weren't at all happy, but the whole thing was a waste of everyone's time and money.

9. The Red Gandhi

Monday, June 15, 2009

We used to play a game called Hands Down. I think Jim had learned it from his older brother Rich. In any case, it was designed as an instructional exercise for new players. If you touched the hack with your hand, which was against the rules, someone had to yell, "Hands down!" and the offender had to put their hand on the ground, and everyone got to throw the hack as hard as they could at their hand. It worked both ways, because often, the thrower would miss.

There was a freshman we knew whom Jim had nicknamed Sandy, because one day he brought in a hack filled with sand. That day, we were playing during our free period—me, Jim, Red, Ox, and Sandy standing in a circle.

Sandy touched the hack. "Hands down!" called Jim. Sandy obediently kneeled on the ground and put his hand down. We all threw the hack at his hand. Ox was the only one who made contact. "Ow," said Sandy.

Jim said, "Oh, shush. This isn't even the one filled with metal ball bearings."

We played for a while longer, and sure enough, Sandy touched the hack again. Jim called hands down again, and Sandy put his hand on the ground. As we attempted to peg his hand with the hack, a monitor appeared out of nowhere. She was an older woman, probably on the wrong side of 70.

"What are you boys doing?" she shouted angrily.

"We're hacking," said Red.

"Well, I saw you throwing a ball at that boy's hand."

"Yes, that's the idea," said Red, and I was relieved he took it upon himself to defend us.

"Is that what you wanted?" she asked Sandy in a probing tone.

Sandy shrugged. "Of course it is," said Red. "It's to teach new players how to play."

"I don't like your sass," she said. "I've a right mind to send you to go see Mrs. Welsh about this."

"Yes, I would love to talk to her," said Red. We were amazed at his brazenness. Mrs. Welsh was the dean of discipline, widely regarded as a bitch.

"Fine, then! Come with me."

"Follow along," Red said to us. "This should be good."

So, we proceeded to Mrs. Welsh's office, the monitor followed by Red, followed by Jim, Ox, Sandy, and me.

The monitor went into her office and spoke to her briefly, then left. She didn't react to the fact that we all stood there to listen in. She left the door open. Red sat across from the dean.

"What's your name?" she yelled.

"Mieczysław Zachariasz Wiśniewski," he said.

"What in the… how do you spell that?"

"M-I-E…"

"Never mind. Mrs. Cea told me you had a boy with his hand on the ground, and you were all throwing a hockey puck at him."

"It wasn't a hockey puck, it was a hacky sack."

"Oh, I don't care what you want to call it!"

"It's not what we want to call it, it's what it is called. You should care, because there's a huge difference."

"I'm not in the mood to argue about semantics!"

"Well, that's too bad, because I am. Semantics are the foothold on the mountain of language. And in the final analysis, my dear, language is all we've got."

"Young man, how dare you?"

"Oh, I dare. Listen, are you familiar with Socrates? He spoke of the examined life. In my opinion, life is much more worthwhile if we consider the merits of its components, such as the game known as Hands Down. Unless you'd prefer to live your life in the shadows of ignorance."

"Get the hell out of here!" She pointed to the door.

"Gladly, my dear." He got up and left. We followed him back out into the parking lot behind the cafeteria, where we hung out during our free period.

For weeks after that, we called him the "Red Gandhi" for standing up to Mrs. Welsh. The funny thing was he never even got in trouble for it.

10. Plano

Saturday, October 16, 2010

I had packed up my car the previous night, after everyone else had gone to bed. I remembered my conversation with Kayla.

"I think not to tell Mom and Dad beforehand is… maybe not the *best* solution, but, well, the least bad one."

I left at 4 a.m. on that autumn morning. At 3 p.m., I stopped in Indiana to eat the lunch I had packed. The bananas had gotten brown and mushy, and my PB&J had gotten sludgy. Oh well. I required sustenance.

I called my mom. She didn't pick up. I left a message: "Hi, Mom. It's 3 o'clock and I'm in Indiana. By the time you get this, I'll probably already be in Plano, Illinois. I've gone to visit Andrea."

I drove the rest of the way. Andrea lived in the suburbs. I got to her door at 6 p.m. Central. I knocked, and a woman I didn't know opened the door.

"You must be Bones!"

"Yes! Forgive me, but who are you?"

"I'm Vanessa. I'm Andrea's partner. Hold on, I'll get her." She ran inside and I heard her yell, "Bones is here!"

Andrea came to the door. "Come inside!" she said warmly, then gave me a big hug.

It was a sensibly decorated apartment. A brown tabby cat walked in. "That's Sneaky McCat," said Vanessa.

"Hold on," I said, "I have to call my mom." I dialed the number, and it rang.

"Jon?"

"Yeah."

"Where are you?"

"Didn't you get my voicemail?"

"No."

"I'm at Andrea's apartment in Illinois."

"Oh. How did you get there?"

"I drove."

"How long did that take?"

"Fifteen hours."

"Why didn't you tell me you were doing this?"

"I didn't know what to do. I didn't think you'd like it, so I asked Kayla—"

"*Kayla* was in on this?" Her tone had gone from concerned to angry.

"She said that's what I should do."

"This is very hurtful, Jon. You should've informed me of your trip."

"I'll be back by the end of the week. Good night." I hung up.

Later, I told Kayla that I believed she had been wrong, and she said, "Well, it wouldn't be the first time I've been wrong."

In the meantime, I sat down at the table with Andrea and Vanessa. "So," Vanessa said brightly, "what are some of your conspiracy theories?"

I was about to laugh, but then I realized she was serious. "I… don't really have any. How about you?"

"You know, I think they're lying to us about gravity. They say it comes from the middle of planets, but I don't know. I think it comes from outside of planets. And they know they're not sure. That's why they call it the *theory* of gravity."

The next day, we drove across town to get pizza, and Vanessa commented on the contrails of passing planes, which she of course thought were "chemtrails." She commented on the government's plot to alter the weather. "What could possibly go wrong?" she wondered.

Andrea showed me her studio. It was a little room she rented a couple blocks away from their apartment. She was working on some very abstract paintings, with deconstructed human beings presented as geometric figures on brightly colored backgrounds. She was talented, for sure.

We played some board games the following day. I told them I liked chess and Scrabble but they didn't have those. Instead, we played others that were pretty dumb.

"So," I said, "any thoughts on the upcoming elections?"

"Oh, we don't vote," said Andrea. "We refuse to participate in a system that doesn't represent us."

"Politics is all controlled by the elites," said Vanessa. "There's no room in it for the rest of us."

"That's it?" I asked. "The elites and the rest of us?"

"That sums it up," she confirmed.

"So what else is there to do here?" I asked. We had mostly been hanging around the apartment the first couple days.

Andrea shrugged. "We're in the suburbs. What do people do in the suburbs?"

"Didn't I see an animal shelter?"

"Oh, Andrea isn't allowed to go there anymore. She always cries the entire way home," said Vanessa.

"What about the movies or something?"

"There's never anything interesting playing."

That night, Andrea asked me, "Would you be all right leaving tomorrow morning?"

"Oh."

"I know we'd discussed a longer stay. But... please don't be offended by this, but I'm getting kind of anxious having you around here. It would be different if we had a dedicated guest room." I'd been sleeping on the living room couch. "I promise you. It's not you."

So, the next morning I repacked my car and got ready to leave. It was about 6 a.m. Central, meaning I would get back around 10 p.m. Eastern. Andrea and Vanessa were in their pajamas. They gave me big hugs as we said good-bye.

After that, my parents left me alone a lot more of the time. I had asserted my independence. I believe this method of parenting is what is known as "giving up." I'd been wandering off my entire life, and now I was wandering into adulthood.

H. OFF THE RADAR

1. Off the Radar

When you're growing up, especially in high school, there's some conjectural ladder of popularity. At the top you have the queen bees, the prom kings and queens, then at the bottom you have the nerds, the kids who get bullied, and then everyone in the middle.

I was not even on that ladder. I was such a misfit I was miles away, making out the ladder in the distance with a pair of binoculars. I believe this was the way Ox felt, too.

2. Susan's House, Part 2

Wednesday, June 16, 2010

I was over at Susan's house for her 51st birthday. Sven, Kayla, Rich, Susan and I were sitting in the circle at the top of the hill, just chitchatting. Suddenly, Sven stood and looked like he had spotted something or someone.

"There's someone with a backpack," he announced. "Oh! It's Red."

Red walked awkwardly up into the circle. "Hey, guys." He took off his backpack and sat in an empty chair.

I said gently, "Red… didn't I tell you this wasn't your scene?"

"Oh, I'm not interested in the Renaissance Faire. I just wanted to see my friends. It's been a while."

It had, in fact, been a whole year.

The party went on as planned, even with this unexpected guest. We ate cake. Eventually, everyone retired to bed, which in our cases were various couches throughout the small house.

When I woke up, I walked to the kitchen, hoping to make breakfast. Red was lying on the floor, right in front of the sink. We tried to wake him, but he was sound asleep. Nobody could make food with him there.

Finally, he woke. "Red, the kitchen floor is *not* an appropriate place to sleep," scolded Rich.

"Ah, sorry," he said. "All the couches were taken."

He went to the bathroom. I used the opportunity to say to Sven, "Please tell that insensitive asshole to leave."

When Red returned, Sven said, "Hey Red, maybe you should get going."

"I'm being asked to leave?" he said, confused.

"Well, everyone's going to be leaving soon," said Susan.

Red hugged Susan good-bye, but it was an incredibly awkward hug.

Once he was gone, Susan said to Sven, "Do me a favor. Let Red know that he's unwelcome here from now on."

He agreed to break the news.

I haven't seen Red since.

3. Elizabeth, Part 1

Monday, October 11, 2010

I was at the café in town. It was somewhere I used to run into Red a very long time ago, but I hadn't seen him there in ages. There was a house guitar, but I'd always been lousy at the guitar.

I sat in one of the chairs, reading, as I usually did. The low din of the customers conversing and drinking their beverages provided a nice backdrop. At one point, an attractive young woman came up to me. "Pardon me," she said, "but are you reading *Gravity's Rainbow*?"

"Yes! Have you read it?"

"I find the ways Pynchon intertwines different plot threads through high and low culture to be scintillating."

My heart skipped a beat. Here was this beautiful woman who also understood postmodernism. "My name is Bones." After my experience at Melville, I didn't bother giving out my real name.

"I'm Elizabeth. Can I buy you a coffee?"

"That would be lovely."

"What would you like?"

"A small almond milk latte, please." She went off to the counter, then returned with my drink and a double espresso for herself. "So, what are you reading these days?" I asked.

"I just started *Foucault's Pendulum* by Umberto Eco. I've heard that *The Da Vinci Code* is the poor man's *Foucault's Pendulum*."

"Oh, absolutely. It's totally comprehensive."

"We should get each other's numbers."

We did, and the next day she called me. "Want to come over this Friday evening?"

I jotted down her address, then drove over when the day came. It was an ordinary-looking house, but I had been directed to the basement, which was accessible from the bottom of the driveway in the back behind the house.

It was early evening. I knocked and she let me in. There were 3 small cats in the entryway. After that was a big room with a small kitchen to the side.

"So, what's your situation here?" I asked.

"I live with my Oma and Opa."

"How do you support yourself?"

"I wait tables at the Thai restaurant in town. I don't have much overhead."

I sat on her bed.

"Care for a beer?" she asked, rummaging through the fridge.

"Sure," I said. I didn't have any idea how old she was, but apparently at least 21. I didn't mention that I was 19.

She handed me a Michelob, then produced a bottle opener and opened it for me, before opening her own. "Cheers," she said, and we clinked bottles.

As we imbibed, we revealed our life stories. She was from New Jersey. Several years ago, her parents had tragically died in a car accident. I said I was sorry; she said it was okay, as it was a long time ago by now. She had moved in with her grandparents, who were from Germany.

I was halfway through my 2nd beer when I said, "You know, for months I've been fantasizing that I'd be reading somewhere in public, and a beautiful woman would come up to me and say, 'Pardon me, but are you reading *Gravity's Rainbow*?' Then I knew she would be the one."

"That's very sweet," she said. I had the feeling she was more sober than I was. "So where did you graduate from?"

I wasn't nearly as drunk as the time with Alexei, but I was a bit buzzed. "Oh, I didn't graduate from anywhere. I went to Melville College in Massachusetts for a year, but it didn't go well."

"Oh."

"How about you?"

"I just finished my BA in English this May at Columbia."

"Impressive. Do you have a lot of debt, then?" I asked.

"No."

"Oh."

"Want to come with me to a reading?"

"A reading of what?"

"Short fiction. A colleague of mine is presenting a new work at Vassar next Saturday. Not tomorrow, but the next one."

"Sounds good. Listen, I should get going."

"I don't think you should. You seem like you've had too much to drink. You can stay here for the night."

She got the bed ready. "Pardon me while I get undressed." She dimmed the lights. Then she slipped off her shirt and pants right in front of me. It was the sexiest thing I had ever seen.

I felt somehow very comfortable in front of her, so I followed suit. I was left in my socks, boxers, and cap.

"Take off that silly thing," she said, and before I could myself, she removed my skull and bones beanie and put it on the night table.

We got into bed. This was my first experience with a woman in this way. "Can I kiss you?" I asked, and we did. "How is this for you?" I asked.

"I like the intimacy. But I don't want to go any further," she said.

"Okay."

Then I passed out.

I awoke the next morning, and she wasn't in bed. I got up and sheepishly put on my clothes. She was dressed too, in the kitchen. "Care for some pancakes?" she asked.

"Yes, that would be lovely."

"You know, they say the first pancake is always a flop. I'll give you the second."

There were two stools at the counter. I sat on one. She delivered me a delicious fresh blueberry pancake with maple syrup on it.

After breakfast, I said, "I should go now." I slipped on my shoes and gave her a long hug. Then I went out through the back door and made my way home. I felt a sense of excitement, but it was tempered by the worry that this was a fleeting thing, something to which I'd be better off attaching no great importance.

4. Poem

Thursday, June 14, 2001

"I think he was being philosophical," my dad said.

"Mr. Bonifacio, I don't think you realize how serious this is," said the principal. "We don't want the community to think we have suicidal 4th graders."

"He's not suicidal," said my mom.

"Maybe not, but he either needs to change the last line, or we cannot publish his poem."

"I know," I said. "I could change it to, '*I wonder what it's like to be in outer space.*'"

"Yes!" said my teacher who was in the meeting. "That's perfect, Jonathan."

So that's what we changed it to. But it was so much more lame than my original line: *I wonder what it's like to be dead.*

5. Elizabeth, Part 2

Saturday, October 16, 2010

Elizabeth's car was in the shop, so she asked me to drive us to Vassar. We got there and there was a room full of well-dressed people, with a table with cheese, olives, and wine. I was hungry, but I tried not to wolf down all the cheese and olives. I didn't have any wine, as I was driving.

Elizabeth introduced me to a woman. "Bones, this is Michaela. Her story, 'Upon Finishing Second in a Foie Gras Eating Contest,' is being published in the *Bailey Review* next month."

I had to assume the title was tongue-in-cheek. I hadn't heard of the *Bailey Review*, but it sounded important.

She looked like she was headed for a fancy party. I shook her hand.

The time came for the reading, and everyone sat down in folding chairs in the next room of the building. A man came to the lectern and introduced Michaela. She had been awarded some fellowship or other.

She read her story. The crowd seemed to enjoy it; they chuckled from time to time. She finished, and everyone applauded heartily. Elizabeth walked around, chatting with various attendees, a cup of wine in her hand.

I felt out of place and awkward. I looked forward to the function ending. Eventually, blessedly, it did. I had parked out front, and we got in the car.

"One second," I said. "I've got to take a piss." I hurried back into the building, found the men's room, and relieved myself. I came back outside. The car was not there.

I was totally confused. I stood there, trying to figure out what happened, when I spotted my car, coming around the block.

Elizabeth was in the driver's seat. "What are you doing?" I asked.

"I'll drive us home," she said.

"Are you sure about that?"

"Yes. Get in."

I got in but soon realized that had been a mistake. She got on the Taconic and started driving wildly. Apparently, she'd had more wine than I'd realized. She wove in and out of traffic, cutting people off, the whole shebang. At one point the car scraped against the guardrail, making an awful sound.

We made it back to her house in one piece. "Elizabeth… how much wine did you have to drink at the reception?"

"Oh, I don't know. A few cups, I guess." Then she started crying. It started as a few tears but quickly became hysterical. I grabbed her and embraced her. Finally, it passed.

"Bones, there's something you should know."

"What's that?"

"I'm seeing someone."

"Oh." My heart sank.

"His name is Greg. He doesn't know about our encounters. I'm so sorry. I don't want to string you along any further."

"Maybe I should leave now," I said.

"Maybe."

I grabbed my keys and headed home.

The next time I visited Kayla, she asked how my car had gotten so scraped up on the side. "The car had an encounter with a guardrail," I said.

"I have to admit, this is kind of frustrating," she said crossly. "I mean, I give you a car, and this is how you treat it?"

"I didn't do it," I said. "My friend Elizabeth did."

"And why were you letting her drive your car?"

"I didn't let her. She took it."

"Then how did you get home?"

"She took it with me in it." I was forced to tell her the whole story, all the gory details. I left nothing out.

"Well, it sounds like I don't need to tell you how *completely* idiotic and unsafe that situation was," she said. "The next time your car is stolen, I'd strongly advise you not to get in."

"I'm sorry." I was.

6. Ox, Part 2

I strongly believe that Ox was a brother to me. I guess I'll never know what it's like to really, truly want to off yourself, but I sure as hell know what it's like to wonder if life is worth it. To have thoughts barreling against your brain like a salvo of bullets, saying, "I'm in so much pain all the time, and I want to die." The difference between him and me is that I always manage to somehow hit the "mute" button until things seem better. There was no "better" for him. There was no rose growing from yesterday's rains. Just a forever of heartache with no exit other than the eternal one.

In that sense, I feel I understood him better now than before he passed. I wish I could have been there for him more than I was.

7. Party

Friday, December 20, 2019

I ran into Amanda and Jack at the pharmacy on an afternoon in December.

"Bones!" Jack said and shook my hand heartily.

"How have you guys been? Are you married yet?"

"Not yet, but soon," said Amanda. "It's going to be in February."

"Oh, good for you." There was an awkward pause.

"Say, are you doing anything Friday night?" asked Jack.

"No. Why? What's up?"

"We're having a party at our house. Want to come?"

"Sure!"

Jack gave me the address and I showed up at the house on Friday evening. It was a genuine house party, the kind I was almost never invited to. I walked in and there was loud music playing, and all sorts of booze was available on the kitchen counter. I wandered around, and it was a veritable who's-who of people I had known a very long time ago. I wondered if Red or Jim would be there, but I didn't spot them.

I poured myself a cup of vodka with coconut liqueur that I'd added. Then I saw Elizabeth. She was chatting with people I didn't recognize.

I went up to her. "Elizabeth!" I shouted over the music. I'm not very good at projecting my voice.

"Bones!" she shouted and gave me a big hug.

"Still dating Greg?"

"No, we broke up many years ago. Listen, I'm sorry about what happened the last time I saw you."

"It's all good. Time heals all wounds and all that."

She went back to chatting with the other folks. I downed the booze and poured myself some more. I wanted to socialize, but I felt like I didn't fit in, like I didn't really know anyone anymore. Maybe I shouldn't have bothered attending parties in the first place. I downed the next cup and poured myself a third.

After the third cup of vodka and liqueur, I felt seriously drunk. Suddenly, I really needed to puke. I ran to the bathroom, but it was occupied. I waited impatiently. At the exact moment that I thought, *If whoever's in there doesn't come out right this instant, I'm going to lose it right here on the carpet,* my old acquaintance Sally opened the door and left.

I ran in, slammed the door, lifted up the toilet seat, and barfed my brains out. It came in several sessions. Finally, gasping for breath, I felt better.

"Amanda!" I shouted over the music. "Thanks for inviting me, but I have to go home now."

"Bones, you've had a lot to drink. I'd feel much more comfortable if you waited. Here, come with me." I followed her into a bedroom. "Just lay down here for a few hours. Maybe you'll fall asleep."

I did. When I woke, I felt sober again. I came back into the house and the music wasn't playing anymore. Only a few people were left. I realized I had been asleep a long time.

"Hey, Bones?" asked Elizabeth, who was still there. "Could you give me a ride home? I'm kind of stuck here."

So I drove her home. Before she got out of the car, I hugged her. Then we kissed.

Amanda and Jack got married 2 months later. I wasn't invited to the wedding.

I. SLACKERDOM

1. Freshman Year

Monday, September 5, 2005

In my school district, 2 middle schools funneled into 1 high school, so when you reached the 9h grade, you were bound to meet new people.

I straggled into freshman English class. It was my first day of high school and I hadn't talked to Will all summer. The teacher was a Mr. Siegemund, a young guy, who looked like he was fresh out of college. I'm pretty sure it was his 1st year on the job. As he explained the syllabus, he paced back and forth like a caged lion, running his hands through his hair. He seemed passionate about language and literature.

"I've assembled a brief questionnaire to get to know you all better," he said near the end of the period. "Why don't you all get into groups of 3 or 4 while you complete it? Then you can get to know each other, too."

The volume picked up from the silence of the teacher's monologue into the buzz of 24 teenagers, trying to find partners for the exercise as the questionnaires were passed out. I sat in the back. I stood and noticed 2 kids sitting in the adjacent corner: One was dressed more or less normally but had bright red hair, and I don't mean red the way a redhead is red, but *red,* like a firetruck. The other was dressed all in black. They were clearly already acquainted. I walked over and introduced myself: "I'm Jonathan."

"I'm Zbigniew, but you can call me Red," said the guy with red hair.

"Connor," said the other quietly. I sat down.

Then another guy approached. "Hey, fellows," he said. "I'm Jim. I'm new in town." To this day, I don't know why he chose to sit with us, but I sure am glad he did. We introduced ourselves again.

The first question asked our names: Jonathan Bonifacio. Zbigniew Wojcik. Connor Byrne. James Paciullo.

"Bonifacio?" asked Jim. "You know, you are pretty bony."

"Yeah. I had my appendix out recently, and I haven't been eating much."

"So maybe we should call you Bones, then."

The second question asked our favorite music. I put down Radiohead. Red put The Doors, Connor put Depeche Mode, and Jim put Queen.

The third and final question asked our favorite book or books. I put down *Lemony Snicket*. Red put *Fahrenheit 451*, Connor put *Nineteen Eighty-Four*, and Jim also put Snicket.

Connor spoke up, "So you guys like Snicket, then. I think it was him who said that one of the great ironies of life is that when a good thing happens to you repeatedly, you get used to it over time, but when a bad thing happens to you repeatedly, it's just as bad every time."

The bell rang, and we all passed in our questionnaires.

As we were leaving the classroom, I caught up with Red. "So how long have you been called Red?"

"I think it started in 7th grade. That's when I started dyeing my hair. Of course, my given name is hopelessly complicated. My dad is Polish. Before I was Red, people usually just called me Z."

"Well, then, you can call me Bones, just like Jim said."

"All right, Bones. Well, a good time for a new name, right? A new year, a new school."

"I'm guessing you already know Connor?"

"I've known him for as long as I can remember. Our mothers were together in the maternity ward, and we live a few houses away from one another."

Within 2 weeks, Jim had everyone calling Connor *Ox*. I asked him what his nickname was, and he just shrugged and said, "Jim. Short for James."

I biked over to the neighborhood in which Red and Ox lived. I'd been invited for dinner at Red's house. I knocked on the door. A more- or less-average looking woman opened up and said, "Well, you must be… *Bones.*" She smiled.

"My name is Jonathan, but you can call me whatever you like. Jon, Jonathan, Bones."

"My son told me that the kids call you Bones, so I'll go with that. Come in, come in."

I entered into a small house. Red sat at the dinner table. He smiled and said, "Hey there. Sit down." I did, and seconds later, Ox burst through the door. "Hi, Rachel," he said.

"Hi, sweetie," she said.

They started talking about music. Apparently Physics Engine had a new album out. It struck me that Ox was more outgoing and talkative here than he was in school.

"Hey," Ox said, "where's your dad?"

"Norm is not here at the moment," said Rachel quietly. We all got the sense that we shouldn't prod. "Anyhow!" She perked up and brought a pot to the table. "Serve yourselves," she said. It was mashed potatoes, and we did. Later, a big bowl came as well that contained peas. It was a simple meal, but hearty.

"So," she said to me. "Tell me about yourself. Tell me about Bones."

"There's really not much to me. I've lived here in Quincy my entire life. I have parents and an older sister. I like to read."

"We like reading too, that is, Ox and me," said Red.

"Yes, I noticed in English class the other week. I can tell you like music, too."

"It's the most important thing for me," said Ox.

"In the world?" I asked.

"In the world," he confirmed. "I mean, I also enjoy other people, like Red and Rachel here. I'm glad to have met you and Jim. Hopefully, I'll know you for a very long time."

"That'll be nice for you all," said Rachel.

There was a long pause.

"Well," I said, dabbing my mouth with my napkin, "I think I'd better get going while it's still light out." I stood.

"See you on Monday?" said Red. "Jim wanted us to all meet up before school by the Four Doors. You know, just to hang out, before first period."

"Sounds good. Thanks for dinner, Mrs. Wojcik."

I headed out.

2. Cart Boy

Thursday, June 9, 2011

In the wake of my exit from Melville College, my parents mostly left me alone. In fact, I was mostly alone in general. Occasionally my mom nagged me about finding a job.

By this time, I hadn't seen Red in about a year, or Jim in 2 years. I still saw Rich occasionally at Susan's house.

One Thursday afternoon, my mom was buying groceries at ShopRite, and I tagged along. "Hey Jon, they're hiring!" she said. "I think you should apply."

So, I asked for an application at the customer service station, filled it out at home, then went back to submit it.

Two days later, I got a call. "Good morning, is this Jonathan Bonifacio?"

"Yes?"

"This is Betty Cooper, calling from ShopRite. We got your application, and we're interested in bringing you in for an interview. Could you come in sometime next week? We could do Monday at 11:30 a.m., or if that doesn't work…"

"Monday at 11:30 works!"

"Great! Just come to customer service and ask for Betty." Betty Cooper, just like in the *Archie* comics.

I drove over in the old car Kayla had given me when I'd graduated high school.

The interview went all right. They asked typical questions, such as a time I had to deal with adversity. I gave total bullshit answers to the best of my ability.

A few days later, I was asked to come in. I stood in the supermarket, wearing pants, a shirt and tie, and an overcoat. "We're going to bring you on," Betty said. I envisioned being a cashier or something. "How would you like to be a cart pusher?" In my head, I screamed, *FUCK!* Instead, I said with a fake cheeriness, "Sure!"

I told my dad about the job. "They're asking you to be a fucking *cart pusher?* I'm sorry, but all the people I see there doing that are clearly developmentally disabled." He walked away muttering, "Cart pusher."

Before I began, I had to complete some training at the corporate office in Poughkeepsie. Among other things, I learned that there were 4 types of shoppers: green, red, blue, and yellow. We also got a fiery speech from the local union head. At one point, we were asked about our hobbies. "I like to read," I said.

"You sound just like my son," said the lady doing the training. "He's always reading."

"That's great!" I said.

"Yeah," she said crossly, "except when it's not, and I have to *punish* him for reading."

My god, I thought, *what a fucking moron.*

My first day, I was scheduled to work from 2 to 8. I got a 20-minute break, which I was required to take because of the union.

It sucked. My job was to retrieve rogue carts from the parking lot and return them to the front of the store. I was also in charge of the bottle machine and had to try to fix it when it broke, which was all the fucking time. During my break, as I ate lunch, two women argued about politics.

The next day my hips hurt like hell. I was scheduled from noon to 6 p.m. At 11:30, I called up customer service and said, "Hello, this is Jonathan Bonifacio. I'm a carriage attendant. I need to inform you of something."

"Wouldn't you like to talk to Betty? She's the one who hired you, ain't she?"

I wanted to say, "Please tell her that I *ain't* going to be working here anymore." Instead, I said, "Just please let her know that due to conflicting responsibilities, I won't be continuing my position at ShopRite."

At noon, my mom said, "Don't you have work today?"

"Yeah," I said. "I'm scheduled from noon to 6 p.m."

"Well, you're late! You have to give them a call!"

"I did call them," I said. "I told them it wasn't going to work out."

"You *quit?*" she said crossly.

"Yes."

"Well, *that* sucks," she yelled. She didn't nag me after that again for a while.

3. Susan's House, Part 3

Friday, August 31, 2018

I was at Susan's house with Kayla. The 2 of us were sitting around the circle with Susan, Sven, and Rich. Birds flitted about the feeders.

"There's something I have to tell you all," said Susan. She paused.

"Yeah?" I asked.

"I'm moving. Sven already knows this."

"Where? Why?" asked Kayla, bewildered.

"I'm going to be joining the Texas Renaissance Faire," said Sven. "I met a guy recently who said that if I join them, they can put me up year-round."

"And with Sven gone, I don't need this house anymore," said Susan. "I'm selling the house and moving farther upstate. I have a place lined up in Greene County." That was far away.

"When are you moving?" I asked.

"Within the month. I'll be busy packing and getting the house ready, so I'm afraid this might be good-bye for our little group."

When it was time to leave, I gave Susan a big hug. "I have something to admit," I said. "I think I always secretly wished you were my mother."

"That's very sweet," she said.

I shook Sven's hand. "Good luck in Texas."

"Thank you, my friend."

I waved good-bye to Rich. That was particularly difficult, as he was my very last tether to Jim, even though I'd probably never see Jim again, anyway.

4. Movies

Friday, January 6, 2006

In early January of freshman year, over Christmas break, Red invited me to the movies. My mom drove me there. It was freezing cold, and I was wrapped in a coat and scarf.

I stood in front of the movie theater, alone. Then I saw two people get out of a car. It was Red and Ox. They approached me, and I gave them hugs.

"Shall we?" I asked.

Red shook his head. "We're waiting for a few more folks to arrive." I imagined he meant Jim, but who else?

Eventually, 3 guys wearing black trench coats traipsed in our direction. One of them sure was Jim. One of the others looked like him, but older and with a waxed mustache, and the 3rd, upon closer inspection, was a young boy.

"I hope it's all right that Matty is tagging along," said the older guy.

"Sorry, but who are you?" I asked.

"Oh. I'm Rich, Jim and Matt's brother."

"Don't worry, they're chill," said Red.

The movie we wanted to see was rated R. "Don't worry, I got this," said Rich. "Don't stand within sight of me until I signal." He disappeared for a few moments, then returned with 6 tickets.

"How did you do that?" I asked.

"I have an ID that's… not exactly accurate. You all can pay me back whenever, by the way."

We filed into the theater and sat in the back row, reminiscent of the back row of the late bus where we hung out after chess club on Fridays after school. We spent the previews and the first 5 minutes of the flick talking and goofing off, before the movie grabbed our attention. It was a stoner flick and very, very funny. Even Matt laughed at the jokes, and he couldn't have been much older than 6 or 7.

Afterward, we went to the Italian place on the other side of the shopping center to get pizza. All in all, it was one of the most memorable nights of that period of my life. The brothers Paciullo lived within walking distance. Red and Ox got rides home from Red's mom. My mom came and got me.

For many years, whenever I happened to visit that shopping center, my heart felt heavy as lead. *Why is this place uninhabited?* I would think. *Where are my friends now?*

5. Tattoo

Tuesday, July 2, 2013

I had a very modest savings account at the bank, from birthday and Christmas money over the years, and the paycheck ShopRite gave me for doing their training and working for that 1 day, which I never spent.

One day, about 4 years after I last saw Jim, I suddenly decided I needed a tattoo. I drove to the place. To get there, I walked behind a building and up a staircase. The House of the Basilisk was wildly decorated. There was a guy hanging out behind the counter. He was huge and absolutely spangled in tattoos, everywhere imaginable. They covered his arms, neck, face, hands, you name it.

"Hey, I called about a tattoo?" I asked.

"What's your name?"

"Name's Bones."

"Oh, right. I'll get the artist. In the meantime, have you got your driver's license?" I produced it from my wallet.

He photocopied it, then yelled down the hallway, "Hey, Christie?" A woman (or was it a man?) hurried in. "Sorry, I've just been having a spot of tea," they said to me in a heavy Cockney accent. "Christie. Christie Sotheby. They/them."

"A pleasure to meet you," I said. "Bones. He/him." We shook hands.

"So, what'll it be today?"

"I want a skull and bones tattoo."

"Just like the name, eh? Any idea where?"

"No idea."

"The stomach is a popular area. Or the chest, although I warn you, that one hurts like hell. Or arms, legs, toes... it's really up to you."

"Okay. How about stomach then?"

They opened a book filled with designs and flipped through it until they found the desired page. "Typical Jolly Roger, then, will it be?" They pointed.

"That looks good."

They took out the design from its plastic sheet, then transferred it into ink on a piece of fabric.

"Step into my office," they said, and I did, and sat.

"This your first tat, then."

"Yep."

"All right, lift up your shirt." They pressed the image onto my stomach, to the left of my navel. "How's that look?"

"Good!"

Then they got out the needle and turned it on. "Don't be nervous, it'll just feel like a pinch."

It hurt a bit, but I was able to withstand it fine. It sort of felt like someone repeatedly stabbing my stomach with a dull pin.

Before too long, Christie was finished. "How's that look, mate?"

"I like it." I smiled.

"Terrific." They wrapped it up in thin plastic and gave me instructions for treating it.

"Hey, darling, it was a pleasure. Come back anytime."

I paid the guy in front and headed out. Bones indeed. Bones on my stomach.

6. Outcasts

Then I found out about Ox. What were we all even doing? Rich had told me a bit about Jim, that he had gone off to college and lived in Maryland, where he worked for a bank. As far as I could tell, Red wasn't up to anything after college. I wasn't up to anything. Ox had been all alone as well. Even Rich wasn't doing much. Why weren't we getting jobs, like normal people were? Were we all part of the new shiftlessness, the 21st century condition of unemployment and slackerdom and poverty and never leaving the nest?

I remembered our last late bus rides in June of senior year after the chess club. We all knew something was ending. How bitter and ironic that there were no new beginnings, nothing to take the place of a halcyon adolescence, spent in the company of fellow outcasts.

7. The Lake and Hephaestus

Wednesday, November 22, 2006

In sophomore year, I had a free period together with Ox, just the two of us. Until then, I didn't feel I really knew him. He was so inside himself all the time. But that year, I saw who he really was.

"Nice weather," I said one day in November. At that point, I knew he was really close with Red, and that made him part of our little group. I felt I should try to be friendly.

"Yes," he said. "Nice weather." A pause. "Hey… would you want to come with me to the lake?" he asked.

"Yeah, that sounds good," I said. It was the first time I had gotten past small talk—a victory.

"Follow me."

We weren't technically allowed to leave campus during school hours, so we walked across the parking lot, behind the music building, up the guardrail, through the jail parking lot, and onto Main Street.

"You know why the jail is right next to the school, don't you?" I asked.

"I'd imagine it's for easy transport of teenage ne'er-do-wells."

"Precisely."

We walked along the sidewalk of Main Street until we came to Lake Drive, where we turned left. There we saw Lake Luddington, a big lake that was shining blue under the blue autumn sky.

"You and I ostensibly see a lake here," said Ox. "But who's to say that it's really there? What if you were the only person in the world who could see a lake, or the color blue? What if all our senses are illusions?"

"I guess you'd still have your thoughts."

"Exactly! Now you get it. In the final analysis, what's in your mind is all you've really got."

"Well, in the meantime, let's enjoy this illusory lake." We stood at the lake's edge in silence for a while.

"It's probably time to get back to school for our next classes," I said, and so we retraced our steps to the cafeteria door. Soon the bell rang.

Another time, I couldn't find him. It was a Friday. I wandered around the parking lot and decided to check behind the music building. There was my friend, crouched and crying.

"Hey, Ox," I said. He looked at me. "What's going on?" I asked.

"We're all going to die," he mumbled through his sobs.

"Well, yes, that's true, but it's not any more true than it was yesterday, and yesterday, you weren't in tears."

"It's Hephaestus. He has a lymphoma in his GI tract. Tonight is his last night to live." That was his dog.

"Oh, I'm sorry." I sat next to him.

"What's the point of living if we're all going to die?" he moaned.

"I admit it, I don't know what the point is. But can't we give death the finger by being determined to live as long as we can and even enjoy it?"

"I don't think I'm enjoying life very much. I'm sorry."

"Well, I enjoy life significantly more with you in it."

"Thanks." He had stopped crying.

"Is there anything I can do? Should I come over this weekend?"

"No. The woman is coming tomorrow morning to put him down. We'll be burying him behind the house."

"I know things seem bleak. But although tonight might be the last night for Hephaestus, there will be many more tomorrows for you. So just remember that you'll always have me, and Red, and Jim, as long as we're around. And that's enough to give life a point to it."

He smiled, a tiny smile, but he smiled.

8. The Future

What would I do with my life? I looked into being a tattoo artist like Christie, but that required lots of art school, and I had no artistic talent. I had tried my hand at liberal arts college but had failed out. I could drum; there was that. Maybe Kayla could get me a job somewhere eventually? She interned for a communications company in the city.

In truth, I didn't know. But somewhere along the way I grew up, something we all did, except for Ox, who never got to. Exactly what I ended up doing is insignificant, only that it involved communications.

PART FOUR: RICHARD

J. GROWING UP CRAZY

1. The Great Event

Tuesday, February 4, 1991

Of course, I remember when my brother Jim was born. In fact, it's one of my earliest memories. I was at the hospital with my parents, my mother very pregnant. My dad went into the room with her as she went into labor. I was kept out of the room to be watched by a nurse. I waited and waited. She gave me candy to help my antsiness.

Then, the great event happened. I was allowed to come into the room at that point, and I saw my brother wrapped up in a blanket, held by my mom, who looked weary but elated. He didn't look like much of anything: a crying pink blob, but that was my new brother and I already loved him. They asked his name for the birth certificate: James Francesco Paciullo, Jr.

I remember very clearly the next conversation that occurred. The doctor talked to my dad about what would happen in the days to come before we could bring him home.

"Of course, he'll be circumcised," said the doctor.

"Like hell he will!" said my dad fiercely.

"Sir, it's for the best. It will be more hygienic, and help protect him from disease later in life."

"So you're going to mutilate my baby's penis because you think I can't teach him to clean behind his foreskin, or use a condom? If you circumcise him, I'll slap you with a malpractice suit so fast your head will spin."

"Okay, easy. We won't touch him then, if that's your wish."

We brought him home after a few days. I had always wanted a little brother and was ecstatic. I promised myself I would always be nice to him and never cruel.

2. Pain

Wednesday, October 11, 2013

I am a liar, a thief, a charlatan, a sadist, and a masochist.

My first memory, outside of Jim's birth, was being at a store with my mom. There was a basket of caramels, and I swiped a few. On the ride home, I carefully unwrapped them and put them in my mouth. Not carefully enough, because she caught me. "I don't want to raise a *thief*," she said.

I've always enjoyed a mild amount of physical pain. It makes me feel alive. The other week, I threw my back out bending over; I mean, the entire lower left quadrant of my back locked up.

I mentioned it to my mom. "Well, what can you *do about that?*" she inquired in an accusatory tone.

"I don't know, take an ibuprofen or something?"

"They're in the cabinet above the stove."

I chose not to take the ibuprofen. Every time I bend backward, the pain shooting down my leg makes me feel a little giddy.

3. Bowling

Sunday, April 4, 1999

When I was in 5th grade, I turned 11. Back when you're a kid, even an older kid, the birthday party is a *sine qua non*, a rite of passage. You get together with a number of ostensible friends for an afternoon and spend time with them as you bask in the glory of being a year older.

My mom took charge of my party: a bowling party. I more or less knew all the other kids who were invited. I got to the alley first with my parents and waited for my friends to arrive.

We were divided into a few lanes. Shortly after we began, I don't remember when, why, or how, I pretended to drop a bowling ball on my foot. Naturally, with a compromised foot, I couldn't bowl. I made a whole show of it, limping around. I'm not sure how realistic the whole thing was.

I think I couldn't possibly allow myself to enjoy myself or have a good time.

On the same note, often when I went somewhere with my parents, when we got back, I would sit in the car, refuse to get out and come back into the house. Just sit there for what felt like hours. I both enjoyed it and didn't, and the enjoyment and non-enjoyment spiraled together, fed off one another, and kept me sitting there until I finally gave in and got out of the car, and came back in.

4. Football

My father often said something about my mother. He said that trying to get validation from her was like Lucy and Charlie Brown with the football. Lucy would hold the football, and say, "Don't worry, Charlie Brown, this time I'll really let you kick it!" But then she would invariably pull it away, every time. Even so, he would go back time and again to try to kick it. That was my mother.

I didn't really understand this until I was much older, like the time I wanted to show her something I'd been learning on the saxophone, and she told me, "Well, you know, you can't *really* play the saxophone." Or the time I tried to tell her that I liked a girl and started by telling her that I didn't want her to make what I was about to say negative, and she declared, "Well, if it's negative, then it's negative." There were countless other examples. When I got to be in my 20s, it hit me like a lightbulb. I suddenly knew exactly what my dad meant. But as he said, you kept trying to kick the football again and again. That was my mom. That was Jocelyn.

5. Music Camp

Friday, July 14, 2000

Long before I ever picked up a guitar, I played mallet percussion. I think I got shepherded into the percussion section of the middle school band because I couldn't get a sound out of a clarinet or flute or trumpet. But it soon became clear that I had a talent with glockenspiels and xylophones, and so I became the unofficial mallet percussionist.

It was a better fate than not being allowed to play the actual snare drum because you were so spectacularly untalented you had to drum on a rubber table instead, which no one in the audience at the concerts could possibly have heard. Everyone can hear a glockenspiel.

I attended a music day camp. I went every afternoon for 2 weeks. I was learning "The Maple Leaf Rag," by Scott Joplin. I've never been very good at reading music, but with the help of the folks who were teaching us, I learned it well.

The time came for the concert. It all went well until my piece. Basically, I panicked. I kept fucking up to the point where I had to retrace my steps with the aid of the piano accompanist. Eventually, I somehow made it to the end.

Everyone said afterward that my piece was their favorite part of the concert. It was another case of self-sabotage: not believing I could possibly succeed at something.

6. Kevin

Friday, April 15, 2022

After Jim came Matt, and then there were 3 of us: myself at 12, Jim at 9, and baby Matty.

Twenty-one years later, Matt was about to graduate from NYU. Jim had long since graduated from Johns Hopkins and lived in Maryland. I was a total failure, about to get into my mid-30s and not up to much, still mooching off my parents. Of course, I had been working part time at the library, but there's not much you can do with a part-time circulation clerk's paycheck, independence wise. At least I had very little overhead.

One day Matt was visiting, as he often did. "Hey, could we have my best friend Kev over sometime for dinner?"

"I don't see why not," said my dad.

"Tell me about him," said my mom.

"Well, fair warning, he's vegan. He also happens to be gay. I know him from the anthropology department."

My dad shrugged. My mom said, "Vegan! I like a challenge. Let's have him over."

We had him over. It went well—*too* well. My mom was very talented at pretending we were a normal, happy family.

At one point during dinner, Kev mentioned that his sister was engaged to Jim's schoolmate, Red. It came as a total surprise to me. Of course, I knew Red, but I didn't say anything.

After dinner, Matt, Kev and I went to Matt's room to hang out. We chatted about music, when Kev asked me if I smoked pot. I said no, not bothering to explain the story of that night with Kayla and Sven. He stayed the night, and I drove him back to the train in the morning.

7. Lunch Bunch

Monday, December 1, 1997

I walked down the elementary school hallway with my dad. We were headed for my 4th grade classroom when we crossed paths with a professionally dressed woman.

"Woah," she said. We turned around. "Where are you headed?"

"I was taking Richard to his classroom. I had to drive him in today."

"My name is Dr. Donato. I can tell something significant is clearly up with you guys this morning. Step into my office. I'll write a note to his teacher."

So, we sat in her office. She explained she was the school social worker. "Tell me, what's your name?" she directed at my dad. "Paciullo." "Okay, then. Mr. Paciullo, could you please tell me why Richard is late for school today?"

"There was… an issue. At home." My dad fidgeted uncomfortably.

"Sir, I assure you, I'm here to help. What kind of issue? Was there a fight?"

"I had to clean up all the broken glass." He sighed. "That she threw at me."

"That *who* threw at you?"

"My wife. I mean, she didn't come close to hitting me. But she was throwing glassware at me, and I had to clean up the broken glass. So, I couldn't walk Richard to the bus, which is why he's late."

That was the reason I attended lunch bunch. I sat in a room with Dr. Donato and a few other kids during lunch instead of the cafeteria. I really don't remember much about it. I remember

that many years later, my mom offhandedly wondered, "Hmm,
I don't remember. Why did Rich start going to lunch bunch?"

8. Kindergarten

Monday, September 10, 1993

I didn't stop my thievery at the caramels. When I got to kindergarten, I decided one day that some of the colorful markers would be better in my possession. I transferred them from the table to my backpack in its cubby as discreetly as I could.

When I finally collected all the ones I wanted, I took them home and removed them from my backpack. "How did you get all those markers?" my mom asked.

"Mrs. Ferguson gave them to me," I lied.

"That was nice of her."

Shortly after that, I had to have a meeting with my parents and the teacher in which I was made to apologize and return the markers. I had my Nintendo privileges revoked indefinitely.

The most important thing that happened to me in kindergarten was that I met Sven and Kayla. The 3 of us became fast friends and playmates. Who's to say how and why little kids become such good friends? But we did.

Pretty soon Kayla and I were invited to Sven's mom's house to play. Her name was Susan, and she was widowed. We found ourselves there often.

By the time I was a teenager, I had practically grown up there. After a while, Kayla's younger brother Jonathan hung out with us, too. When Jon got to high school, he became friends with my brother Jim, and Jim joined us as well. At one point, Sven wanted to meet Jon and Jim's friend Red, although Red wasn't really his name, and he wouldn't tell us what it was, only that it was complicated and started with a letter near the end of the alphabet.

Susan's house was a respite for me from the dysfunction of

my own household. Anytime I needed a break, I'd ask permission
for a ride over to Susan's.

9. Connecticut

2009

We had lived in Quincy since I was born, and that's where Jim and I went to grade school. Shortly after Jim graduated from high school, my dad got a new job, and my parents had to move the family to Connecticut. Jim rarely came back after he left for college, though, so that left Matt in a new middle school, and me, with our parents, who were somehow still married.

10. Ganja, Part 2

Friday, July 25, 2003

"I bought some from Carissa," said Kayla. "We can do it in the park," She had gotten a hold of a little plastic box of marijuana, bud, ganja. We were 15. "Are you down?"

"I'm down," said Sven. "Rich?"

"Sure. I'm down."

We waited until nightfall. Then we snuck into the park after hours, climbing the wire fence. It was easy: The fence wasn't very tall.

It was a summer evening, finally dark, but still pleasant. Sven had brought a flashlight. We stood beneath a big tree.

"Want to do the honors?" he asked Kayla.

He shone the flashlight on her as she packed the drug into a small pipe, then pulled out a Bic. She lit the grass and took a breath in. She held the smoke in for a good 10 seconds, then exhaled.

"How does it feel?" asked Sven.

"Really good. Peaceful." She passed the pipe and lighter to him and he followed suit. Then came my turn. I was worried I'd have a coughing fit, so I measured my breath carefully. It worked—no coughing.

We passed the pipe around one more time before the stuff was exhausted. That had been enough. We were totally stoned. For the longest time we just stood there. Crickets were chirping in the summer night.

Suddenly Sven asked, "Why does anything exist?"

"Hmm?" said Kayla.

"I just mean… I exist here, but what if nothing else exists but the little point between my eyes? Hey, do I have my wallet with me? I have it. Yes. Wait a minute… what was I just talking about?"

"You were talking about existence," I said.

"That's right. So, what if I never amount to anything? I mean, what if I can't hold down a job or things like that? Oh, God."

"What?" Kayla said.

"What if I'm gay? What if I take advantage of some kid someday while he's sleeping?" He suddenly shook all over. "I can see… geometry…"

"I think you're having a bad trip," I said. I could barely hold a solid stream of consciousness together myself, but that much I could tell.

He crouched down, then toppled over. Finally, his breathing returned to normal as he fell asleep.

"What do we do with him?" asked Kayla.

"We should wake him, and get him home."

I shook his shoulders. "Sven?"

He opened his eyes, and said quietly, "Geometry…" Then he fell back asleep.

"All right," I said to Kayla. "Let's do this."

I heaved Sven's body up with all my might, and we balanced him on our shoulders. We dragged him as far as the fence.

I shook him violently this time, and he opened his eyes again.

"We're going to get you home. But we need you to make it over this fence. Do you think you can do that?"

He mumbled something. Then he climbed the fence successfully, and we followed him over. He was still semiconscious.

"Come on, buddy," I said.

We walked together to Susan's house and deposited him there. We figured it would be up to him to explain to his mother what he was doing asleep outside their front door.

After that, I swore to myself I'd never smoke marijuana again.

Many years later, Jim started doing it, and then Matt confided in me he was interested. He said Jim would smoke him up. I told him that I wouldn't necessarily recommend it, but I could claim no real moral high ground on the matter.

11. Meds

Thursday, November 21, 2002

One day in 9th grade, I took the bus home from school. I had a small sewing kit on me, for whatever reason. I sat next to this older preppy girl, Laura, whom I found incredibly annoying. She wore a halter top that exposed her midriff. I decided I needed to stab her with a pin. I pulled it out of the kit, and feeling completely emotionally numb, save for a bit of satisfaction, inserted it into her back.

She jumped. "Ow, fuck! What the fuck was that?" It bled a little where I had stabbed her, and the sight of the blood intoxicated me. "Was that you, you little shit?" Her stop was coming up, and the bus slowed down. She got off the bus in a huff.

When my stop came, before I got off, the driver told me, "You know, Rich, I saw what happened with Laura, and I have to report you to the principal, because if I don't, and her father calls tomorrow and complains you stuck her with a pin, I'll be the one who gets in trouble."

I sat with the principal and my dad.

"Mr. Paciullo, I'm looking over your son's record. It looks like he was under the supervision of the social worker at the elementary school."

"That's right."

"It isn't normal to think you can go around sticking people with pins. He's a young man and ought to know better." The man took off his glasses and wiped his brow with his sleeve, then replaced them and continued. "I have a number for a doctor I think you should seriously consider seeing. If you take him, I can avoid having to discipline him for this incident."

So, I sat with my dad in the office of Dr. Jan Higgins. It

was comfortable, with many framed diplomas on the wall. She insisted I call her Jan. We went over my entire history, and it was a bit alarming, to me, to my dad, and to Jan. The stealing, the lying, the social difficulties, the self-destructive behavior, and general lack of being well-adjusted.

"Mr. Paciullo…"

"Please. Call me Jamie."

"Jamie, I believe your son may be on the autism spectrum. This by no means needs to be a debilitating condition. There are many people with autism who have perfectly productive and fulfilling lives. I'd like for him to try a medication."

I started taking haloperidol. It helped, I guess. I saw Jan once a month from then on. Many years later when I turned 26, she wrote a very dire sounding letter to whomever oversees such things to keep me on my parents' insurance. And then again when I turned 29. And again when I turned 32.

12. Baseball, Hacky Sack and Girls

Monday, February 7, 2005

There was a question I often asked myself growing up and into my adolescence, which was, *Why the fuck is it that life comes so incredibly easy for everyone else?*

I played baseball from when I was a little kid until I was in 6th grade, after which my mother took me off the team because of my poor grades. Years later, she offhandedly asked me, "Hey Rich, why was it that you stopped playing baseball?"

I was spectacularly untalented, and in my last year I was on the worst team in the league. We never practiced. Sometimes they put me in right field, but most of the time I wasn't even allowed in the field due to there being too many kids on the team. When I came to bat, my opponents would yell, "Easy out," and the outfielders moved in. Frankly, it didn't matter what they did, because I couldn't even get the ball to the outfield.

I had one glorious day. Somebody finally convinced them to let me play second base. I successfully fielded a grounder and threw it to first in time and then caught a popup. Later in the game, the unthinkable happened: I got an infield hit. I made it to first, but then I turned the base the wrong way, and the first baseman pretended to throw the ball back to the pitcher but did not, and he tagged me out. The ump made the indication, and I was in disbelief. I stood there next to first base, and I started crying. Somebody yelled, "You're *out!*" Finally, I staggered back to the dugout.

When I got to 9th grade, I learned how to play hacky sack. There was a senior named Jeremy who was an absolute wizard at it. He could stall it on his feet, his knee, the top of his head, and so on. He could kick it behind him, swivel around and kick it again, and swivel around to kick it once more. He could even do the legendary "double dragon," which consisted of jumping in the air and kicking it between one's legs, landing, and then doing it again before the hack hit the ground. He told me once that I should practice on my own, just kicking it over and over again, and once I could do it 100 times in a row it meant I was good. Eventually, I could do it.

Jeremy also taught us a game called Hands Down, which was to teach new players not to touch the hack with their hands. If you slipped up and touched it, you had to put your hand on the ground, and everyone else got to try to spike you with it, although most people usually missed.

There was a girl I really liked in high school named Zoë. She was on my bus: I think she had been friends with Laura once upon a time. I got the feeling she might have liked me too, although I very well may have invented it.

In the 11th grade, Zoë suddenly stopped coming to school one week. I mentioned to my mom I hadn't seen her all week, and she found out through the grapevine that Zoë had pancreatic cancer. I called up her mom and asked if I could maybe visit her the next time she was home from the hospital.

I opened the door, and she greeted me. Her head was totally shaved. She seemed weak but otherwise more or less herself. We decided to watch a movie. It was her favorite—*Young Frankenstein.*

As I sat next to her, I thought to myself this was the most beautiful girl I had ever seen. It didn't matter that she was without any hair. I wanted to kiss her badly, but I couldn't work up the courage to make a move. After the movie ended, we sat there for a while.

As it turned out, that was the last time I ever saw her, because she succumbed to her illness not long after. The whole thing was brutally swift.

13. Jim and Matt

Thank God, Jim and Matt turned out a lot more normal than me. Being a total failure at everything else, I devoted my energies to being the best big brother I could be.

I think it turned out to be a noble pursuit. It's not unlike the mother who stays home with her children full time. Our actual mother was so emotionally absent, most of the time it was up to me to fulfill that role.

K. THE ALBUM

1. Music

Wednesday, April 4, 2001

"Happy birthday, Rich," my dad said. I opened the 1st gift. It was a Walkman. The 2nd one was a bit bulkier. "What could this be?" I said, smiling. It was what I expected: a nice pair of headphones. "And the last one," my dad said. "You're 13 years old now, and it's time you explore the world of rock 'n' roll." He handed the third gift to me. I knew it was a CD. I opened it. "*A Night at the Opera*," I said. "By Queen."

"This album changed my life," he said.

I sat on my bed with my Walkman and headphones. I popped in the CD and pressed play. The first track was called "Death on Two Legs."

Freddie's piano intro began, followed by Brian's guitar effects. The instruments wailed together until they suddenly cut off and the song began.

"You suck my blood like a leech, you break the law and you breach, you screw my brain till it hurts, you're taking all my money and you want more..."

I listened in awe. So, this was rock and roll. Heavy metal, even. I *liked* it. It was, so far, the greatest epiphany of my life.

I saved my allowance money to buy more albums. I didn't know what to look for, being without the benefit of an older sibling or friend. My dad said he could offer some suggestions, but he emphasized it was my journey. He told me I should talk to the people at the record store.

I walked in and went up to a guy who was organizing the LPs.

"Hi," I said. "I'm Rich."

"Jesse," he said. "Need any help finding something?"

"Well, that's why I'm talking to you. I've been listening to *A Night at the Opera* by Queen, and I really like it."

"Hmm. How much money do you have?"

I dug around in my pocket. "Eighteen dollars and twenty-five cents."

"What part of the album do you like?"

I thought. "I really like the sound. I like the guitar solos."

"You should listen to *Queen II* and *Sheer Heart Attack*, both also by Queen. If you're ever interested in branching out, come back here and we can talk again."

So, I bought those two albums. I barely had enough money.

I sat on my bed again to listen to my new purchases. They both blew my mind. *A Night at the Opera* was good, really good, but those 2 albums were on another level. To this day, they're 2 of my all-time favorites.

The next time I visited Jesse at the record store, I thanked him heartily for his recommendations and told him I wanted to branch out.

"What direction do you want to branch out into?" he asked. "Queen are basically progressive metal. We could go in the progressive direction, or the metal direction."

"How about both?" I asked. "I have enough money for two more albums."

"All right. Wait here." He went rummaging through the stacks of CDs and came back with 2. He handed them to me.

"*In a Glass House* by Gentle Giant, and *Scream Bloody Gore* by Death," I read.

"Be forewarned, these 2 albums could not be more different. But they should give you a better picture of what kind of music you'd like to explore."

As it turned out, I loved them both in different ways. Gentle Giant were incredibly cerebral and challenging, whereas Death were an assault. Nonetheless, I found them incredibly relaxing. When I listened to Death, it pushed everything else out of my mind, all my anxieties and worries.

One day my dad and I visited the music store down the road from the record store. In the back was a whole wall of guitars, of many shapes and sizes.

"Looking for a new instrument?" the guy asked.

"I don't know," I said. "I've only ever played mallet percussion."

"Well, you're welcome to try out a guitar."

"How about that one?" I pointed to a beautiful blue guitar with two points at the bottom, the kind a glam rocker might play.

"Sure." He plugged it into a small amp and tuned it, and then he handed it over to me.

I sat down. I'd never touched a guitar before. I played with the strings. I decided to try to play the harmonized guitar solo from "Lazing on a Sunday Afternoon," the Queen song from *A Night at the Opera*.

To this day I don't know how, but I played it. The guy stared in disbelief. "You've never played a guitar before?"

"Nope."

"Sir," he said to my dad, "your son has a gift. I highly recommend he continue to hone his considerable skill."

My dad bought me the blue guitar and a pack of 10 lessons as an advanced Christmas gift. Very advanced, as it was July.

I played the guitar all the time. I tried to play all the songs I could. I didn't know how I did it, but I could listen to a song and play it.

The lessons went all right. The teacher, Mr. Chu, told me on the 1st day that my playing was very sound, and the best he could do for me was to work on advanced topics, such as solo technique. Then he asked if I'd written any songs.

"I haven't," I said.

"Well, would you like to?"

"Sure."

"Let's focus on that, then."

Over the next 10 weeks, I learned about music theory and
songwriting. I started to understand how I was playing what I
played. I also learned how to write some of my own solos. At the
end, Mr. Chu said, "I believe I've taught you everything I can. Go
forth and make music."

I had found my calling.

2. Library

Friday, January 4, 2008

"You know, you have quite a bit of leisure time," my mom said.

"Well, it doesn't feel fucking leisurely," I shot back. The next day, I apologized. "I'm sorry I cursed at you."

"I forgive you, but you need to find something to occupy your time with. You've been out of high school for a full year and a half now. And I know you like spending time with Kayla, Sven, Jim, and Jonathan. But there's life outside of that. You need to become a productive member of society. You have to. That's how it works."

A few days later she showed me the *Pennysaver*. "Hey, Rich, the library is hiring. That's just down the road."

I called them to inquire, and they asked a few questions: Did I have a high school diploma, could I lift 25 pounds, did I have transportation? They asked me to come in the next day for an interview.

Bundled in my winter coat, I walked into the parking lot and a car window lowered. There was a woman with short hair and glasses.

"Please tell me you're Rich," she said in a heavy Bronx accent.

"That's me," I said.

"The building is closed. The heat's broken. Hop into my car."

I obeyed and got in the passenger seat. It was nice and warm.

"All right. My name is Maude. Rich, we are desperate for help. We need someone to start right away. We'll pay you $8 an hour. Can you come in on Monday? How does noon to 4 sound?"

"Sounds fine to me," I said, and I showed up the next day at noon.

"Rich, the dumbwaiter is *chaos*," Maude said. That was the

dumbwaiter that carried books between the adult collection on the ground floor, and the children's room on the second floor. It was my job to empty the dumbwaiter and shelve all the children's books. It was a long and tedious task, but it also brought a certain satisfaction once it was all done.

The important part as far as I was concerned was the paycheck. After working there for 2 weeks, I received a check for $500.

I went to the bank and set up a checking account. They even gave me a debit card.

Pretty soon, I was able to afford a solo recording kit.

3. Making the Album

By the time I was 16 years old, I had written about 10 songs. I decided I needed to make The Album. It would be a solo project, under the name Decibel Ordinance. The album would be called *Noise Code*. I realize now that that was a bit redundant.

Once I was 19, I became obsessed with the album project. It was my *raison d'être,* my purpose in life. I knew that if I could make it, I would become rich and famous, but that was not why I wanted to do it. I wanted to be respected as an artist.

I spent countless hours holed up in my room, recording guitar parts and vocals. But I could never get it right, could never solidify my vision for the album.

As time went on and my 20s passed me by, I gradually realized that the album would never be complete. The vision faded. I was doomed to be an ordinary human being who happened to be able to play the guitar.

4. Physics Engine

Friday, October 16, 2020

Maude quit after one year. I had overheard her in her office with the business lady, Alexa, complaining about how much she hated attending board meetings.

Our circulation manager, Janice, became the interim director.

One day before that happened, during my regular shift, I had taken my lunch break. Sitting at a table in the community room, I took out my haloperidol and took my usual dose. Then I rested my head on my arms. I was very tired for some reason.

I must have fallen asleep, because I felt my shoulders being gently shaken, and a kind female voice saying, "Richard, people don't need to see your medication."

One day soon after, Janice took me aside. "Rich, do you remember me?" she smiled and asked.

"Do I remember you? Uh… well, you've been working here a long time, right?"

"Your mother took you here for storytime when you were very small. I was a volunteer then. I practically remember when you were born."

"Oh, wow."

"Do you realize what happened the other day? The library board held a meeting in the community room. They walked in there and saw an employee with his head down and a bottle of pills in front of him. That looked bad. In fact, Maude was ready to fire you. I told her to give you another chance."

"Wow. I'm sorry. And thank you."

"Anyhow, when I heard that you were interested in working here, I told Maude we needed to hire you. And since you've been doing such a good job in the children's room, I'd like you to move downstairs and become a circulation clerk."

"Does that pay more?"

"I'm afraid not. I wish I could say yes, but our budget is so tight. But you'll get to work with the public more. Trust me, it's a step up."

Pretty soon, we had a new director, Diane. She was a lot younger than Maude. She was nice and seemed to like me. Our library was the kind where if you want to be director, it's either your first gig or your last gig. It was not exactly a prestigious position.

So now I was a circulation clerk. They got someone new to be dumbwaiter wrangler. I liked the work: I checked books in and out, placed and sorted holds, and called patrons to remind them to return items, among other things. I still made $8 an hour.

The years went by and eventually I got a raise to match inflation: $10 an hour. I saved all my money at the bank. It was very abstract to me, because I had such little overhead. As far as I was concerned, I could have written a massive check and given it to Matt for all I cared. I spent money on music. Pretty soon, I had a huge collection of CDs. I liked all sorts of genres, but particularly prog rock and metal.

My favorite band was a group called Physics Engine. They were a progressive metal band out of Boston, all virtuosos at their instruments, who had studied at Berklee. In 1999, they released their debut album, *The Black Device*. It was my favorite recording ever, and I listened to it all the time.

I remained acquaintances with Jesse from the record store. One day, he mentioned to me that they had an opening for some hours on Sundays. My library job was Monday, Thursday, Friday, Saturday, so I accepted. The record store paid a whopping $16 an hour.

I was 31, and the pandemic hit. The record store closed indefinitely. The library shut down its brick-and-mortar operation, but they remained open online and kept me on to monitor the chat feature. Basically I sat practicing the guitar and answered the occasional question that someone submitted and got paid for it. It was a pretty good gig.

By that time, Diane wasn't director anymore. We had gone from her to Jill to Tammie.

I received an email one day from Tammie:

"Dear Richard,

I hope this note finds you well. I appreciate your taking the time to monitor our online service.

I was thinking that it would be great if you could offer a program this summer and/or autumn via Zoom. It could be any topic you choose. You would devise it, present it, and evaluate it.

Let me know your thoughts.

Tammie Dupont"

At first, I wasn't so sure about it. What could I possibly offer the community? *Think,* I told myself. *What do you know a lot about? Of course! Rock music.*

I responded to the email.

"Hi Tammie,

I'd like to offer a Remote Rock Music Appreciation Club. It will run 8 sessions, every other week from July to November. I'll lead participants through the history of rock music and explain the chain of influence. We'll explore various genres and learn about the subject through sample songs I will assign.

Rich"

She liked the idea. We advertised the program online on the website and Facebook page. By the time it was about to begin, I had 7 registrants.

It went well and mostly as planned. For each session, I assigned music and then I lectured about it, followed by a discussion.

During our discussion of '90s metal, one of my participants, Cole, asked offhand, "Hey, Rich, have you ever heard of the band Physics Engine?"

"Yes, they're one of my favorite bands of all time."

"Do you know their guitarist, Adam Reid? He's my brother-in-law."

I was stunned. "Are you serious?"

"He's married to my sister. Maybe I could get him in on one of our Zoom sessions."

Cole asked later if he could give Adam my email address. "Of course," I said.

I received an email the next day from Adam himself.

"Hey, Rich!

The boys and I are busy recording right now, but I was thinking we could do a one-on-one type thing together, and you could share it with your group."

Then he gave me his phone number. I couldn't believe it. I had Adam Reid's personal email address and phone number.

I texted him about doing a Zoom interview and if I could record it, and he said yes. We set up a time, and it came. I had a list of questions prepared, but it ended up being more like a conversation. The interview went great. He felt like an old friend.

I asked him if I could share it with the world at large, and he said, "You're welcome to do with it whatever you'd like, my friend."

I eagerly uploaded the recording to YouTube. Then I hurried to Physics Engine's official online forum, registered an account, and made a post with the heading, "My Interview with ADAM REID," and the body: "Today I had the immense pleasure of interviewing Adam Reid," and I linked to the video.

I waited for the responses to come in. They did, and it was a disaster:

"Very awkward interviewer," said the first response.

"Interviewer was awkward as fuck, but it was nice of Adam to go along with the guy and make the best of it," said the second.

"Next time you interview someone, if you do it again, you might want to have a list of questions prepared to streamline the process or maybe consider transcribing the interview to get rid of that awkwardness," said the third. Okay, a little more helpful at least.

Everyone seemed to share a similar sentiment. I wrote, "I had a list of questions prepared. And I know I'm awkward, I'm sorry."

Someone was kind enough to write back, "Don't be sorry, man. We're trying to help you. And for what it's worth, I enjoyed the interview. It was a fun conversation."

I was so disappointed that my interview didn't garner a more positive response. Here I was, as knowledgeable about Physics Engine and progressive metal as anyone on the planet, and my efforts to pass on some of that knowledge were completely unappreciated.

At least the Zoom group seemed to like it.

5. Justin

Friday, May 12, 2023

There was a kid who started coming into the record store around the time I turned 35. His name was Justin. He was tall and had very long brown hair. He sometimes asked me for recommendations. Of course, I told him he should listen to Physics Engine. He bought a vinyl copy of *The Black Device*.

The next time he came in, I asked, "So, what did you think?"

He shrugged. "It seemed to me to obfuscate for the sake of obfuscating."

"You didn't like the arrangements?"

"I found them hopelessly complex."

I was disappointed. Naturally, since I loved Physics Engine, I wanted everyone else to love them, too. I gave him some other recommendations of less complicated music of a similar genre.

He came in and said, "I listened to *A Night at the Opera*."

"Oh, yeah?"

"Yeah, and that's what I'm talking about!"

"Great! I should've started you off with that in the first place."

It struck me I would enjoy seeing Justin outside of the record store, but I was worried it might be awkward due to the age difference. I never got his number.

6. Wine

Saturday, August 31, 2019

Tammie asked me to weed the cookbooks. I felt so bad doing it.
I basically decimated our wine section. I mean, no one had been
taking them out, and we needed room for new ones, but still,
they were beautiful books.

7. Tara

Saturday, July 5, 2014

When I was 26, I bought my first car. It was a blue 1999 Cadillac Seville and cheap, though it had a lot of miles on it. I didn't plan to drive it that much.

Matt was 14, and a freshman in high school. Every morning, I'd wake up and give him a ride to school, which he thought was the coolest thing ever. Depending on my work schedule, I'd pick him up too, or he'd have to take the bus. It was only about a ten minute drive.

There was a good family friend named Tara. She lived near San Francisco, so I hardly ever got to see her. Since I had accumulated a huge amount of PTO at the library, and it was easy for me to take days off at the record store, that summer I hatched a plan to take a road trip to California to see Tara.

My dad encouraged the idea. He told me stories of hitchhiking to Tucson, Arizona, when he was barely 18, playing harmonica and singing in bands for drinks and women.

My mom was totally lukewarm. "I know you'd like to see Tara," she said, "but couldn't you fly?"" The answer was simple: Driving is an adventure; flying is a pain in the ass.

Tara said I could stay at her house for a week. I was very excited: I had never been west of Pennsylvania before. I packed up my car with some of my belongings, including my blue guitar and a small amp. I also packed a ton of snacks for the road.

There's something incredibly profound about getting in a car and knowing you're going to be in it for 14 hours. It's not at all like how I imagined being in an airplane would be—the tedium of being stuck in your seat at the mercy of the pilot as you floated above the clouds. When you're in a car, you're the pilot. You're in control. Every road sign you pass is a milestone toward progress, physical and spiritual movement.

I got up at 4 a.m. just before the sun rose, got in the driver's seat of my car, and exhaled. I turned the key. The old car shuddered to life.

I drove. I took Route 7 north to I-84 and headed west. I had a huge box of CDs in the passenger seat to listen to during my journey. When you're on a long road trip, albums go by fast. I did not get bored. The day went by, and I didn't stop for meals. I occasionally pulled off the highway to eat one of the snacks I had packed. Pretty soon, it was 8 p.m., and I was in Illinois somewhere. I found a cheap motel.

"I need a room. Nonsmoking."

I paid and headed to my room with my suitcase. The whole process was very efficient. That was Thursday night. I had brought my CBD oil for relaxation. It had the side effect of making me sleep less, which was ideal for a long road trip when it is best to be up and out by 4 a.m.

Here was my driving schedule:
Thursday: Norwalk, CT → Joliet, IL
Friday: Joliet, IL → Potter, NE
Saturday: Potter, NE → Elko, NV
Sunday: Elko, NV → Piedmont, CA

I arrived at Tara's at 3 p.m. Pacific Time. I pulled into the parking lot of her apartment building, walked up the stairs and knocked.

She opened the door. "Rich!"

I gave her a hug, then kissed her on the cheek. She pulled back and said, "Ooh… you have stubble. Girls have sensitive skin."

I followed her in. "Here's some hand sanitizer," she said, pointing to a bottle, which I used.

Her apartment was totally white. The carpets, the counters,

    INSTANT REPLAYS OF THE EXODUS

the walls… all white. Then a black cat rounded the corner and meowed.

"This is Mikolas," she said. I approached him but he growled and hissed and turned back the other way. "Okay," I said, "never mind."

"Sorry," she said. "He can be a bit skittish. You probably need to decompress," she continued. She directed me to a tiny room in the back of the apartment that had been outfitted with a bed.

I took a long nap. When I woke up, she said that I must be hungry and prepared eggs for us. I sat at the table and began to eat.

"Rich!" she scolded. "It's impolite to eat that fast. And don't smack your lips, either. Eat like a human being. It might seem petty, but it's not."

"Sorry," I said.

"It's okay," she said. "I'm just letting you know so you know how to act around people."

She was unmarried. I figured she was retired and had a pension or something.

The next morning, I pulled my mustache wax out of my things and waxed my mustache, as I was fond of doing. I brushed my long hair out, parted in the middle. I walked into the living room.

Tara stared at me. "What's with the hair and the mustache? You look like an applicant for a Black Sabbath cover band. I know you like 70s rock music, but *no, danger, Will Robinson.*"

I trudged back to the bathroom in embarrassment, washed the wax out of my mustache, and pulled back my hair.

"That's much better," she said, smiling.

It felt so good to have made it to California. I felt a strong sense of accomplishment.

"So, what would you like to do while you're here?" she asked. "Of course, I'll show you around. There are some hip restaurants and shopping. And we'll go into San Francisco a couple of times."

"I don't know," I said. "I just want to hang out here and be, if you know what I mean."

"Yeah, I totally get that."

That afternoon we walked into Piedmont. It was very pedestrian friendly. The weather was beautiful and there were many people strolling about.

"Here, I'll buy you a wheatgrass shot," she said at a vendor, and she handed it to me.

I looked at it.

"You drink it. It's like a shot of alcohol."

"A shot of alcohol?"

"Sure! Haven't you ever had a shot of alcohol? Like, at a party?"

"I… don't really get invited to parties," I stammered, feeling ashamed. I gulped the wheatgrass down.

It was a nice town.

A couple days later, we took a bus to Golden Gate Park in San Francisco. We walked around and then visited the de Young Museum. It was a beautiful place. We were looking at the paintings in the museum, when I asked Tara offhandedly, "So, how long have you had Mikolas?"

"Rich," she scolded. "When I'm doing something, I like to do just that one thing. Right now, we're looking at paintings."

The next evening, we were hanging out at her apartment. She'd had a couple of glasses of wine. She said, "You know, you have a receding hairline, and you're developing a bald spot."

"Yeah…?" I said, embarrassed.

"You should read some men's style magazines to figure out something else to do with your hair. Your current style is not very flattering."

"Okay."

We went into San Francisco again the next day, this time visiting Chinatown, which was fun. The next day, I told her I was going to head out the following morning.

I packed my things and loaded up my car. She followed me into the parking lot. "Give me a hug," she said, and I did, and I didn't try to kiss her this time. Then I got in the car and left.

8. CBD

Thursday, July 10, 2014

"Richard, you been smoking a little bit of weed?"

"No, sir."

"You been around someone who's been smoking a little bit of weed?"

"No, sir."

"Well, if you're being untruthful with me, and I search your car, and I find something, that's when I put people in jail."

"I understand, but I'm telling you the truth."

I was sitting in the officer's passenger seat. After having pulled me over, he invited me in to chat. He sniffed the air as if he smelled something. I remained silent. Then he asked, "What have you got in that there bag?"

I opened my messenger bag. "Well, my wallet, and…"

"What's that?" He pointed at my CBD bottle.

"Well, that's CBD. It helps with anxiety."

He grabbed it. "Hoo-whee, what have we here?"

"Sir, it's perfectly legal."

"I'll be the judge of that. Get out of the car and put your hands up."

I obeyed. Before I knew it, I was being handcuffed and having my Miranda rights read to me. I was escorted into the back seat of the vehicle, and we drove to the police station. I was put in a holding cell.

I saw the officer who had pulled me over in conversation with a couple of other officers. Then he was on the phone for a very long time. Finally, about an hour later, he opened the cell door and unlocked my handcuffs.

"You're free," he said. "Here's your bottle." He handed me

my CBD. "And your bag." He handed me my messenger bag.

"Bill?" he shouted. Another officer appeared from a door. "Will you get this kid back to his car?"

Bill drove me back to the side of the highway where my car was. "Son, I'm sorry you had to go through that," he said. "Drive carefully, okay? If you hadn't been following the car in front of you so closely, we wouldn't have pulled you over in the first place."

I had a hunch that it had more to do with my old car with New York plates and my long hair.

I got home a few days later without further incident.

L. REUNIONS

1. Reconnection

Saturday, February 29, 2020

Jim was here for a wedding. His old friends Jack and Amanda were getting married.

"How'd it go?" I asked him when he got home.

"You'll never believe what happened. I saw Red!"

"Whoa. That's a blast from the past."

"Honestly, I didn't think I'd ever see him again. I was so bad to him and Ox and Bones after high school. I realize now that I totally abandoned them." He sighed. "I wonder how they're all doing."

A week later, Jim was about to leave when he came into the house, waving something. "I got a letter! From Zbigniew Wojcik! That's Red!"

He quickly wrote a response, stuffed it into an envelope, applied a stamp, and put it in the mailbox.

A few days later, another letter came. Jim was back in Maryland, so I called him on the phone and asked permission to open it and read it to him. He acquiesced.

It said that his friend Ox was dead. Suicide, a number of years ago. Jim was silent. Then he wept. "Oh, if only I had known. If only I could have been there." He sucked back his tears. "I guess it makes sense. He was always so sad, so reserved." He sighed. "God damn. If only there were a way we could all give him a proper send-off. But it's too late now."

Or is it? I thought. Then I hatched the beginnings of a plan.

2. Dissociation

Wednesday, March 27, 2024

I find it unbelievable, unfathomable, that, in my 30s, I've experienced everything I've experienced, yet I'm still young.

I'm about to turn 36. The mirror is unfaithful to reality. It must be. I'm just a soul. This body beginning to age is not me.

I float through the days. I don't know what it means to be human. Sometimes I feel most comfortable in oblivion. Oblivion is safe and warm.

3. Kayla

Sunday, May 5, 2024

I looked in my phone contacts under K. There it was. Kayla. I opened my text conversation with her, and it had been many years. I felt it would be impolite to text her, so I worked up the courage to call her.

It rang four times. I was sure it would go to voicemail, when I heard a familiar voice. "Hello?"

"Kayla?"

"Yes, who is this?"

"It's Rich Paciullo. Remember me?"

"Of course! How the hell are you?"

"I'm so-so. Listen, there's something I desperately need to ask you. But I'd prefer not to do it crudely. Where are you located?"

"Manhattan. You?"

"Connecticut. Can we meet up somewhere? I can come into the city."

We set up a time on a Sunday afternoon. I drove to the train station and took the New Haven Line into Grand Central. Then I took the 6 downtown, *way* downtown, to Bowling Green, practically to the harbor. I walked up to the street, then followed my phone's GPS to the restaurant. As I meandered along looking for the place, I heard, "Richard!"

I turned around and there was my friend. She was dressed professionally, with a short, smart haircut. She smiled broadly and opened her arms. I hugged her.

"Over here," she said, and led me to the entrance. It was a bowl place. We picked our meals, and she insisted on paying. We sat down. "So, what have you been up to?" she asked.

"Embarrassingly little. I work at a library and a record store.

I live with my parents. There's an album I've always wanted to make, but I never will." I shrugged.

"Well, you can't always measure success traditionally. I'm sure you're good for something, if you think hard enough."

"I believe I have the respect of my brothers."

"Hey, that's super important! Richie, you're a good bean. We need people like you."

"So, what are you up to?"

"I'm a communications specialist for a cable television provider."

"Wow. Sounds high-powered. But I never doubted you. I'm proud of you, Kayla."

"Thanks, sweetheart." There was a moment of silence that wasn't awkward, instead rather tender. "So, there was something you needed to ask?" she asked.

"Yes. Do you have an address for your brother?"

"Jonathan? Sure."

"Can you text it to me?"

"Sure, no problem. Why, are you going to show up at his door or something?" She was kidding.

"No. I just need to send him something. It's super important."

"He's working for my company, too. I got him an internship, and afterward, they hired him."

"Oh, that's good to hear. I was just going to ask how he was. What about Sven? Have you been in touch with him?"

"I've totally fallen out of touch with Sven. After he moved to Texas, he sort of disappeared."

"And what about Susan?"

"Again, no idea. It's funny, in this modern world you'd think it'd be easy to keep track of people all the time. But it's really not true."

"It's hard to make new friends, don't you find? Once you get into your mid-20s and early- to mid-30s."

"You're 36 now, right? Me too. Yeah, it's hard. The people I most interact with are my coworkers. Richie, I spend so much time working. But that seems to be the way of the world, doesn't it? You grow up: yes, you resist it, but you grow up, and then you work until you're old. All of society is a massive waiting room for retirement."

"I might shave my head."

"Seriously?"

"Yeah. I have a receding hairline and a bald spot."

"You've had long hair ever since I can remember, which is a very, very long time."

"Well, anyhow, I should get going. I'd like to catch the 3 o'clock train home from Grand Central."

"Okay. Well, I'm so glad you got in touch, Richie. Let's meet again sometime."

"For sure."

We got up from the table and exited the restaurant. We had a nice long hug, then we went our separate ways.

I got a text: Jonathan's address. Now I could at last put the plan in motion, the one I'd been hatching for 4 years, the one I had kept procrastinating on, but was finally fulfilling.

4. Novel

Monday, June 19, 2024

"You've been writing up a storm," said Annie.

"I think I've finally finished it," said Red. "My life's work. I don't know if I'll ever write another novel, or maybe not for a very long time. I've kind of exhausted my life experience for this."

"*Instant Replays from the Exodus*," she said.

"Actually, I changed it back to *of.* Instant Replays *of* the Exodus. It sounds more powerful that way. I don't care if it's pretentious."

5. Ox's Birthday

Sunday, June 23, 2024

"Hello?"

"Hey, Jim! This is your brother, Richard."

"Oh, hey, Rich! What's up?"

"There's something I need to ask. Remember your friend Ox?"

"Yeah, of course. Why?"

"When was his birthday?"

"August 1. Why?"

"August 1. What year?"

"1991. Again, why?"

"I was just wondering. Thanks. Bye."

6. Postcards

Monday July 1, 2024

Jim was at the post office checking his P.O. box. There was a postcard there. It was from Quincy, New York. There was a type-written message that read:

"Dear Jim,

I request your presence at the Quincy Diner, 2 pm, August 1, 2024, to celebrate my birthday.

—Ox

P.S. Bring the music."

He was dumbfounded. Ox was dead. Clearly someone else was masquerading as him. But he realized that whatever was going on was important and made plans to appear as invited.

Jonathan checked his apartment building mailbox. There was a postcard there. It was from Quincy, New York. There was a typewritten message that read:

"Dear Bones,

I request your presence at the Quincy Diner, 2 p.m., August 1, 2024, to celebrate my birthday.

—Ox

P.S. Bring a balloon and Sharpie."

That was a month from now. It couldn't be Ox. Whatever was happening, though, he would for sure be there to find out.

Zbigniew checked the mailbox of his late mother's house. There was a postcard there. It was from Quincy, New York. There was a typewritten message that read:

"Dear Red,

I request your presence at the Quincy Diner, 2 p.m., August 1, 2024, to celebrate my birthday.

—Ox

P.S. Bring a hat."

A hat? What in the world was going on? Ox had been gone for a decade. He wanted to know what would occur at the diner, though, so he planned to show up.

7. Birthday Party

Thursday, August 1, 2024

It was August 1st. Jim sat at a booth in the Quincy Diner. He had with him an old iPod and 2 speakers. He wasn't sure what to expect: Was Ox's ghost going to appear or something? Then he spotted a guy walking in. He had red dyed hair. He approached the booth where Jim sat.

"Jim," he said.

"Red. It's really you."

Red sat next to Jim and hugged him. His face collapsed into Jim's shoulder. They remained that way for a long time. Then they were interrupted by a voice.

"Fellows."

They looked up.

"Bones," said Jim. "Get over here." Then the three of them had a group hug.

"Red, I'm so sorry for what happened over at Susan's house," said Bones. "It was all so long ago. I couldn't bear not to forgive you now. You're my friend."

"I'm sorry, too," said Red. "I like to think I've grown a lot as a person since the last time we met."

"I'm certain we both have," said Bones.

"So," said Jim. "Ox's birthday."

"Ox would've been 33 today," said Red. "You know, it's been 10 years now since he's been gone."

"I don't know who gathered us, but they asked me to bring a balloon and a Sharpie. I don't know why," said Bones.

"And they asked me to bring a hat," said Red.

"Hey, can I see that balloon and Sharpie?" asked Jim.

Bones gave them to him, and he blew up the balloon and tied

it. Then he took the marker and drew a face on it.

"Give me that hat," Jim asked Red. He took the porkpie hat and put it on top of the balloon. Then he took 4 saltshakers and used them to anchor the balloon.

"I present Ox. Our friend."

Everyone smiled.

Jim sang, "Happy birthday to you, happy birthday to you! Happy birthday, dear Ox, happy birthday to you! May you live 100 years, may you drink 1 million beers! Get plastered, you bastard, happy birthday to you!"

Red started to cry. Bones patted him on the back. "There, there."

Red composed himself. Then he said, "I finished a novel recently. It's called *Instant Replays of the Exodus*. It's about you guys. And Ox."

"I hope I'm portrayed kindly," said Jim.

"As kindly as possible. Jim, you're legendary in my book. Do you know how much I miss those days? Going to chess club and then taking the late bus? I think we as humans are damned to nostalgia like that. I believe that all of life consists of desperately searching for lost Edens."

"I miss it too, man. It was a powerful feeling, being respected by my peers. When I went off to college, it was totally different. I was just a little fish in an ocean of other fish."

"You went to a big college, right?"

"Yes. A university."

"I went to a small liberal arts college. The best thing I can say about it is that's where I met Annie."

"Oh, that was that girl you were at Amanda and Jack's wedding with, right?"

"Yeah. We're engaged now."

"Congrats!" said Bones. "I'm totally single."

"That's too bad," said Red.

"It's okay. I don't think I need to be in a relationship to be happy. I used to think that. But not anymore."

"What about you?" Red directed at Jim.

"Yeah, I've got a girlfriend. Her name is Krystal. No plans to get married just yet, though."

The waiter took their orders. Jim ordered a cheeseburger and a soda. Bones ordered a stack of waffles. Red ordered a portobello wrap and a black coffee.

"So, about Ox," said Red. "This may be a birthday party, but it's also the closest thing we may ever have to a funeral. I don't know if you know this, but Colleen and I scattered his ashes together in their backyard after he passed. So, I'd like to say a few words."

He cleared his throat. "There once was a boy named Connor. Connor never really fit in anywhere he went. He immersed himself in music to distract from the pain he constantly felt, the pain he didn't think anyone else knew about or could understand. When Connor got to high school, he met a guy named Jim Paciullo. Jim called him Awks, or Ox, because he was the awkward one in his group of friends. Connor, Ox, that is, made it through high school on the strength of Jim's kindness, as well as the support of his best childhood friend, Zbigniew Wojcik, also known as Red, and their other friend Jonathan Bonifacio, also known as Bones.

"After high school, he found the time ahead to be a deep, dark pit of despair. He didn't see any way out of this toxic cloud. Eventually, he couldn't take it anymore and decided the world would be better off without him, or perhaps he would be better off without the world. And that is the condensed story of Connor 'Ox' Byrne. Let's remember him and his story."

They were silent for a few moments. Then their food came. They didn't speak as they ate, either.

"Maybe this doesn't have to be the end for Ox, in a sense," said Jim. "If we gather here every year on August 1st, he'll live on that way."

"I like that idea," said Red.

"Yeah," said Bones, smiling. "Me, too."

"So, I couldn't help but notice the speakers," said Red to Jim.

"Do you know what it's time for?" he asked.

"'Fat Bottomed Girls'?" said Bones.

Jim nodded. "'Fat Bottomed Girls.'"

He queued up the song and played it as loudly as would be polite in a public space. Finally, the moment came. Brian May's guitar paused. And Jim shouted in unison with Freddie, "GET ON YOUR BIKES AND RIDE!"

The song ended, and the three of them sat there, content. Then they all stood.

"Well then, my friends, until next year," said Jim. as they walked into the parking lot. "Two p.m., same spot."

"You got it," said Bones.

"So long, my dear friends," said Red, and then they each got in their cars and drove their separate ways.

8. Shaving My Head

Friday, August 2, 2024

"Hey, Rich. Thanks for organizing the party," said Jim.

"So you knew it was me all along?" I asked.

"Of course!" said Jim. "You had just asked me about Ox's birthday. It was obvious. The balloon and marker and hat were brilliant. I can't thank you enough."

"Well, I do what I can."

"In fact," he continued, "we've decided to make it an annual thing."

"Ah. That warms my heart. Truly."

The next day, Jim drove back to Maryland.

I stood in the bathroom. I lifted the front of my hair. There was less hair there than 10 years ago, that was for sure. Then I grabbed the hand mirror and turned around. I had a bald spot, no question. Trying to cover it up or hide it seemed dishonest. So I placed a trash can under myself, took the electric clippers to my head and shaved it all off.

I looked in the mirror. Of course, I still didn't see any "me" there, but I felt a bit better about things. Long hair was something for Young Richard. I was not young anymore.

Matt was the only one of us who was still truly young, at 24. I decided to call him.

"Hello?"

"Hey, Matty. It's Richard."

"Oh, hey! How's it going?"

"Not bad. You know, Jim was here for a few days."

"Oh, nice. I haven't seen him in a while."

"Matt, you're still young. I want you to savor the hell out of it. When you're my age, I want you to think, 'Yes, those days are long gone, but I sure as fuck enjoyed them as they were passing me by.'"

"What brought on the philosophy?"

"It's something I've been thinking about lately. The best you can hope is that you get to be my age and think these things. You know, not everyone gets to."

"Why? Do you think I'm suicidal or something?"

"Not you, Matty, not you."

"All right. I have to go. I'll talk to you later, Rich." He hung up.

Matt lived in a studio apartment in the Bronx with his best friend Kevin. Kevin was a graduate student in anthropology and made some money as a TA, and Matt worked for Trader Joe's.

9. Onwards

20??

Of course, 36 becomes 46, which becomes 56, and on and on and on. The best we can do is understand that these things are illusions, like our reflections in the mirror. Maybe the world is an illusion, like how when you look at a blue lake, you might be the only person seeing blue or a lake.

Somehow, though, those of us who are determined to stay alive do it. In our mind's eye we capture those fleeting moments of our flight from the trials of life, like instant replays of the exodus.

Acknowledgments

Thanks to Bill, Barbara, Robin, Dave and Jacob for all your support. Thanks to Justin. Thanks to Kelsey and Roxxy. Thanks to my editor, Jeannine. Thanks to my designer, David. Thanks to Kris for being the first person to encourage my writing. Thanks to the Unfortunates. Last but not least, thanks to all the dumpster kids I hung out with in high school.